NURSE

C000119611

75p

Haven't you got a young man yet? That's all Nurse Helena Chamberlain hears from her match-making Aunt Norah. Helena daren't admit that she is hopelessly in love with inaccessible surgeon Miles Tracy, for just one hint, and Aunt Norah would interfere. And that would be a disaster . . . Or would it?

*Books you will enjoy
in our Doctor Nurse series*

HEARTACHE IN HARLEY STREET by Sonia Deane
DOCTOR ON THE NIGHT TRAIN by Elizabeth Petty
LOVE ME AGAIN by Alexandra Scott
A MODEL NURSE by Sarah Franklin
NURSE ON THE SCENE by Lindsay Hicks
ISLAND DOCTOR by Clare Lavenham
TABITHA IN MOONLIGHT by Betty Neels
MARINA'S SISTER by Barbara Perkins
EXAMINE MY HEART, DOCTOR by Lisa Cooper
INTENSIVE AFFAIR by Ann Jennings
NURSE IN DOUBT by Denise Robertson
ITALIAN NURSE by Lydia Balmain
PRODIGAL DOCTOR by Lynne Collins
THE HEALING PROCESS by Grace Read
DREAMS ARE FOR TOMORROW by Frances Crowne
LIFE LINES by Meg Wisgate
DOCTOR MATTHEW by Hazel Fisher
NURSE FROM THE GLENS by Elisabeth Scott
SISTER STEPHANIE'S WARD by Helen Upshall
SISTER IN HONG KONG by Margaret Barker
THE CAUTIOUS HEART by Judith Worthy
THE PROFESSOR'S DAUGHTER by Leonie Craig
A SURGEON'S LIFE by Elizabeth Harrison

NURSE HELENA'S ROMANCE

BY

RHONA TREZISE

MILLS & BOON LIMITED
15–16 BROOK'S MEWS
LONDON W1A 1DR

All the characters in this book have no existence outside the imagination of the Author, and have no relation whatsoever to anyone bearing the same name or names. They are not even distantly inspired by any individual known or unknown to the Author, and all the incidents are pure invention.

The text of this publication or any part thereof may not be reproduced or transmitted in any form or by any means, electronic or mechanical, including photocopying, recording, storage in an information retrieval system, or otherwise, without the written permission of the publisher.

This book is sold subject to the condition that it shall not, by way of trade or otherwise, be lent, resold, hired out or otherwise circulated without the prior consent of the publisher in any form of binding or cover other than that in which it is published and without a similar condition including this condition being imposed on the subsequent purchaser.

*First published in Great Britain
by Mills & Boon Limited*

© Rhona Trezise 1984

*Australian copyright 1984
Philippine copyright 1984
This edition 1984*

ISBN 0 263 74850 2

Set in 11 on 12 pt Linotron Times
03–1084–46,000

*Photoset by Rowland Phototypesetting Ltd
Bury St Edmunds, Suffolk
Made and printed in Great Britain by
Richard Clay (The Chaucer Press) Ltd
Bungay, Suffolk*

CHAPTER ONE

STAFF NURSE Lester and Nurse Chamberlain wheeled the medicine trolley into the ward and stopped at the bed just inside the door. Nurse Lester unhooked the chart from the end of the bed and was reading it.

'How are you feeling today, Mrs Bride?' she boomed.

The patient shook her head. 'Not too good, I'm afraid.'

Nurse Lester took a bottle of tablets, extracted four of them, placed them on a tray and held them for Nurse Chamberlain to check, then entered the dosage on the chart. Helena Chamberlain took them to the patient, said she hoped they would do the trick, then they moved on to the next bed.

Miss Quick, a thin, anaemic-looking woman who was in for observation, complained bitterly of a headache which had troubled her all night and kept her awake. She was given a mild pain-killer and the fact was noted.

Mrs Bloom, who had been admitted after having fallen against a heavy steel cabinet in her office, was coughing breathlessly and had a hand pressed against her ribs.

'Can you give me something for my cough, Nurse? I feel exhausted.'

Nurse Lester looked at her searchingly through

her spectacles and said in an undertone to Helena, 'She's always complaining about something but they haven't been able to find any reason as yet. I'm inclined to think she's neurotic but there's always the chance something is wrong so we will have her with us for some time yet.'

She raised her voice. 'I'm sorry, Mrs Bloom, but I haven't any cough mixture. Have a word with the doctor when he comes round.'

Mrs Powell was recovering from a recent abdominal operation and needed a gentle laxative. Nurse Lester poured a thick white liquid into a plastic medicine cup.

'Cheers,' Helena said brightly as she handed it to the patient.

'Thank you, Nurse, it's good to see a pretty, smiling young face for a change. Nurse Lester scares me to death,' Mrs Powell said in a whisper that could be plainly heard.

Nurse Lester stiffened, then turned and glared at them both with round, gooseberry green eyes.

'Hurry up, Nurse, this is supposed to be a medicine round, not a chat show.'

With her large, brawny arms she pushed the trolley farther along the ward. Helena's short-sleeved green and white check dress swung from side to side, revealing long, shapely legs as she hurried to rejoin her. The black belt beneath the crisp white apron accentuated her tiny waist, and on her short, light brown curly hair a small white tucked cap was pinned precariously.

There was an air of unrest and anxiety in the ward as patients with 'nil by mouth' notices pinned on the wall over their beds waited to be taken to the theatre for surgery. Because of industrial action by the ancillary workers, some patients who had been prepared for theatre were not sure that their operations were deemed to be of sufficient importance to be dealt with. As hour followed hour they looked anxiously towards the ward doors whenever they heard the sound of an approaching trolley. Gradually they became tired and dispirited.

'Do you think they'll be doing me today, Staff?' Mrs Penfold, the patient in the end bed asked on a sigh.

'And how am I supposed to answer that?' Nurse Lester demanded. Her sandy hair was scraped back so fiercely from her forehead that her eyes bulged. 'They don't let me into their secrets.'

'But I'm so thirsty! How soon will it be before I can give up all thoughts of having my op and get a cup of tea?' pleaded Mrs Penfold.

'A couple of hours, I should think. You ought to be very thankful that your gall-bladder is not considered urgent enough to be dealt with as an emergency. You should count your blessings, Mrs Penfold.' The nurse moved across the ward on flat feet.

When they had completed the medicine round they wheeled the trolley outside and padlocked it to a pillar. Nurse Lester marched purposefully into Sister's office and picked up the telephone receiver.

After a few minutes she came out and said balefully, 'There's no joy there, they won't commit themselves. But if you ask me, none of our lot will be done today. Come on, we'll get a cup of tea while the going's good.'

This was Helena's first week at Trelawny hospital which was situated in the far south-west of Cornwall. Compared with St Ann's in London where she had trained, it was unbelievably small, more like a cottage hospital. St Ann's was like a town with its huge out-patients' block, chest clinic, dentistry department, medical and nursing schools, X-ray department, pharmacy, occupational therapy unit and shop which sold the articles made by patients, as well as the vast rooms where the medical records were kept. Helena thought with amusement of her early days there, when she had frequently lost her way in the labyrinth of corridors.

Here there was no fear of that. Even the wards were not segregated, medical and surgical cases occupying, where possible, opposite ends of the same ward.

At St Ann's you looked out on tall, grimy buildings dirtied by the fumes of passing traffic. Here, the view from the windows was an expanse of fields and trees and, in the distance, the sea. And all that dirtied the buildings were the droppings of seagulls.

At St Ann's the consultants had their own dining-room with waiter service and the sisters had a room apart from the junior nurses. Here at Trelawny there was just the one dining-room and although, generally speaking, each group kept to its own kind, that was not always so.

Each ward had its own kitchen and Helena went in there now to put on the kettle.

'Do we use proper tea or tea-bags?' she asked.

Nurse Lester sat on a stool which she overlapped. Her outstretched legs and feet in lace-up shoes looked enormous.

'One tea-bag will be plenty.'

Helena leaned against the old-fashioned, shabby sink as she waited for the kettle to boil.

'It's rotten for the patients waiting for their ops, isn't it? I should think the waiting is even worse than the real thing,' she said.

'Huh! Most of them were petrified at the thought of having an operation and certainly weren't anxious to have it done. Now, to hear them grumbling, you'd think it was the thing they wanted most in life! And their relations ring up and demand to know why it's been put off as if they can't wait to get them under the surgeon's knife,' Nurse Lester sniffed.

'But you can understand it. I wonder if we would be any different?'

'Probably not. But you can't help feeling impatient with some of them,' Nurse Lester said flatly.

'Do you take sugar, Staff?' Helena asked as she placed the mug on the table beside her.

'No thanks.' She sipped the hot drink gratefully. 'For every patient in here there are many more at home awaiting admission. There's a list as long as your arm. I should think it would take years to clear the backlog.'

'The surgeons must get very fed up about it. It's almost as bad for them as for the patients,' Helena mused.

Staff Nurse Lester nodded. 'Very frustrating. They know that a condition which seems fairly routine can prove to be much more serious and treating it in time is all important. It could mean the difference between life and death. Still, there's nothing we can do about it, except to make sure that the patients don't feel too sorry for themselves because that can only do them harm. Mr Tracy is most anxious they are kept in good spirits.'

'Is he the chief surgeon?'

'Yes. Mr Miles Tracy,' said Staff Nurse Lester.

'I've never met a Miles before.'

'He's a real charmer.'

'I do believe you've got your eye on him,' Helena teased.

'Me? You've got to be joking. Why would I want to do that? I've got a husband of my own, and a son in Australia. And if you take my advice you won't fall for him either, because you'd be fighting a losing battle. You'd be at the bottom of a list headed by Sister Bell. He wouldn't be interested in anyone lower in rank than that.'

'Sister Bell? I think I saw her the day I came here. Has she got pretty dark hair and brown eyes?'

Nurse Lester nodded. 'She's sweet enough when he's around but she's very strict with her staff. You'll want to watch out for her.'

'That doesn't worry me. I like a sister to be a good disciplinarian. Some of the new ones at St Ann's were too easy-going in my opinion.'

'Mr Tracy is a disciplinarian and it certainly hasn't affected his popularity. All the staff, and the patients too, dote on him.'

'Poor man, fancy having to put up with that! I bet there's some jealousy, too.'

'You can say that again! But you don't have to waste any pity on him, he laps it all up. He knows he has only got to lift a finger or an eyebrow to have every female come running.'

'And yet he isn't married, apparently?' Helena asked disbelievingly.

Nurse Lester shook her head. 'What about you? Have you got a young man or are you still looking?'

Helena laughed. 'Neither. I've recently done a stint in Men's Surgical and since then I've thought of them as anything but glamorous.'

'Oh, so you don't like to think of men being human and having prostates and hernias?'

'We-ell, I don't think I would fall in love with a patient, let's put it that way. But if I met a man and he became ill afterwards, that would be different,' Helena replied.

'You're a romantic, and I predict you will fall hook, line and sinker for Mr Tracy. So don't come crying to me, saying I didn't warn you.'

'Don't worry, I won't do that. I'm not keen on the sort of man who knows that he is every girl's heart-throb.'

A satirical gleam came into Nurse Lester's eyes. 'What brought you down here? I should have thought there would be more going on in London for a girl like you.'

'I suppose that's true, and I'm very fond of London. But my father is an engineer and he and Mother have gone to Kuwait because he has a contract there. I was living at home because the residence was full at St Ann's and it would have meant me trying to find digs, which isn't easy at the price I could afford to pay. So I came down here because this vacancy included accommodation. And it happens to be near where my aunt lives.'

There was the sound of a trolley being wheeled along the corridor. Staff Nurse Lester rose to her feet.

'Come on, Nurse, that will be Mrs Cooper back from theatre.'

A porter, nurse and houseman wheeled in the still unconscious woman on a stretcher trolley.

'Set up a saline drip, Staff, and take half-hourly checks night and day, please. It wasn't as straight-forward an op as we had hoped,' Dr Jones said.

Nurse Lester glanced around the ward. 'In that case we'll have her over there in the corner bed because we will need to have the light on all night. We don't want to disturb the other patients, or night staff won't be very pleased.'

The telephone rang in Sister's office and as Sister Bell was on sick leave Nurse Lester went to answer the call. 'Wheel Mrs Penfold over here and put Mrs Cooper in her place, Nurse. And see to the drip,' she said as she hurried away.

'Am I going for my op now?' Mrs Penfold asked hopefully as Helena and the porter did the change-over.

'Not as far as I know,' Helena said.

'No, you won't be having it done today, they've finished operating. You've got a reprieve,' the porter said.

Mrs Penfold gave an angry, exasperated sigh. 'I don't want a reprieve, as you call it, I want my operation. You lot ought to be here where we are, waiting and waiting, with nothing to eat or drink, expecting to go for it any minute and nothing happening. I don't think you've got any hearts.'

'Don't carry on to me, missus! *I'm* working, aren't I?' he said huffily as he walked away.

'Cheer up, Mrs Penfold,' Helena said in a comforting voice. 'This means you can have something to eat and drink now. What about a nice boiled egg?'

'Bless you, Nurse, that sounds marvellous. But mostly I'd like a nice hot cup of tea, I'm that thirsty.'

'Right you are. How many minutes do you like your egg?'

'Four minutes, dear. Oh I'm so glad you're on duty, Nurse. I'm sure that other one would have left me to wait till supper time.'

When Helena had checked the drip for Mrs Cooper she went into the kitchen and prepared a tray for Mrs Penfold, keeping her fingers crossed that Staff Nurse Lester would not be back in time to raise any objections. Luck was with her, for she heard the telephone ring again.

'There you are, I've cut your bread and butter into soldiers so that you can dip them in the yolk. I loved doing that as a child, did you?' Helena asked as she adjusted the pillows and saw that Mrs Penfold was comfortable.

The woman's eyes filled with easy tears of weakness. 'You're an angel, you really are.' She grabbed one of Helena's hands and squeezed it hard.

'I've been called many things in my time, but never an angel! Just you wait until you know me better,' Helena grinned and went to answer another patient's call.

Nurse Lester was kept busy in the office. Helena and Nurse Jelbart fetched bedpans, changed sheets and made up beds for the patients who were still in the recovery room. Mrs Cooper was moaning feebly as the effects of the anaesthetic wore off. Nearby patients eyed her with morbid fascination, no doubt thinking that as she was now, so they would be in the course of the next few days. Helena went to check that she had no untoward symptoms and that her drip was functioning correctly.

'All right, Mrs Cooper, it's all over. You are back in the ward. Mrs Cooper? Mrs Cooper?' Helena said in a loud voice to bring her back to the present.

'I'm cold, my feet are cold,' she murmured indistinctly.

Helena fetched another blanket and tucked it around her legs. 'That's better, isn't it?'

The bell rang to warn them that supper was ready in the food trolley in the lift. Staff Nurse Lester came out of the office and went into the kitchen to serve the individual portions and Helena and Nurse Jelbart took them into the ward. The smell of minced meat was strong and some of the patients complained that they had had it the day before. That was true, but the kitchen staff were working to rule and nurses were providing whatever was available.

No sooner was supper cleared away and patients made comfortable again than more visitors arrived carrying bunches of flowers, ranging from the simplest home-grown to handsome cellophane-wrapped bouquets. They took stools from under the beds and walked self-consciously to the end of the ward to fetch more. Conversation grew louder and was punctuated by bouts of coughing or moans from the more ill patients.

When the visitors had left, vases had to be found for the flowers and bowls for fruit. Personal items such as clean nightdresses, talcum powder and tissues had to somehow be squeezed into the tiny lockers. Wrapping paper was taken away and fresh drinking-water was placed on locker tops. Pillows were plumped up and sheets straightened. Then came the hot drinks round and the oft-repeated question, 'Horlicks, milk, Bovril, cocoa, Ovaltine?'

'You'd better go for your supper break now, Nurse Chamberlain,' Staff Nurse Lester said at last.

As Helena made her way along the covered walk to the dining-room, her mind was on the unexpected severity of Mrs Cooper's operation and the discomfort she was suffering. She had seemed particularly well beforehand, which underlined the difficulty of deciding when an operation was urgent. As she pushed open the swing-door she collided with someone who was coming out.

'Oh, I'm sorry,' she said, looking up apologetically. 'We've already got enough patients without me trying to provide another one!'

The man stood aside to allow her to pass. They looked at each other for a brief, hypnotic moment, when his grey eyes crinkled into a smile which Helena found irresistible. He was nearly six foot tall, with broad shoulders. Brown hair which sprang crisply from his forehead had a slight wave in it and a sprinkling of silver. The face was rugged with a square jaw.

'I don't believe I could be hospitalised so easily,' he said, his mouth turning down at the corners as if to contradict the smile in his eyes.

His voice was resonant, coming from the head rather than from the throat. It fascinated her and she wanted to hear him speak again. Then she realised that not only was she staring at him but she was also blocking his path.

She moved aside with a little laugh. 'I'm sorry.'

'Thank you, Nurse.'

She watched him stride away, looking lithe and casual in a brown corduroy jacket over light brown slacks. He inclined his head to two young nurses who passed him on their way to the dining-room.

As Helena waited at the counter for an egg on toast, the two nurses brought their trays and queued behind her. Helena turned to them and introduced herself.

'We are Collins and Coe,' the elder of the two said. 'I'm Collins.'

'Nice to meet you both. Which wards are you on?'

'I'm in Maternity.'

'And I'm in Casualty,' Nurse Coe said.

'I rather liked the spell I did in Casualty at St Ann's. It's always full of interest, isn't it?' Helena smiled.

'True, but a bit gory.'

'So is Maternity,' Collins grinned. 'Where are you?'

'In General, under Sister Bell.'

'That's where Staff Nurse Lester is. She's a bit of a martinet, but a good nurse.'

After a moment Helena said, 'Who was that very good-looking man in the cord jacket who passed you just now?'

'That was the Casanova of Trelawny, Mr Miles Tracy,' Collins said.

So that was the man who Staff Nurse Lester had warned her about. It was as well she had done so, for he had undoubtedly attracted her. Now she would be on her guard, for nothing would induce her to fall a victim to his charms. But how well she could imagine that he would cause feminine hearts to flutter.

'I heard that he and Sister Bell were . . .' Helena looked at them questioningly.

'Well, the betting is on her at the moment, but very long odds. I don't think I'd risk my ten pence on anything coming of it, he's doing very nicely as he is. Like a pop star, he would lose a lot of admirers if he got married, and that wouldn't please him at all.'

'What about you two? Are you both keen on him as well?'

They exchanged glances. 'There would be something wrong with us if we weren't. But we are only junior nurses and he doesn't even know of our existence. You have to admit he is very dishy.'

'Mmm, if you like that type of man. Personally I prefer fair men,' Helena lied.

'She'd like Bill then, wouldn't she, Coe?' Collins said smoothly.

Coe shot her a dark look.

'Who's Bill?' Helena responded.

'That's Dr Wood. He is younger and slimmer. Tall, fair hair, and very keen on nurses—he eats them for breakfast!'

'He has the bluest eyes,' Coe said dreamily.

'Crumbs! You are lucky down here with two such eligible doctors. We didn't have anything like that in London. Are you both Cornish?'

'Yes. We're both from Wadebridge, that's north Cornwall. I'd hate to leave Cornwall.'

'And this hospital?'

'Definitely this hospital.'

Helena's half-hour supper break was over and she still had an hour of hard work ahead of her before the night staff came on duty. She had reports to write up for Staff Nurse Lester, and another medicine round which was chiefly to give out sleeping-pills. She stood and watched while the patients swallowed them, for there was to be no possible chance of a depressed patient hoarding them until she had a fatal dose in her possession.

Bedpans had to be given out, drips laid ready for replacement during the night, and a final look at each patient as they settled down. Then the lights were switched off, with the exception of the large, dimmed one over the ward doors and the one over Mrs Cooper's bed.

Helena said goodnight to Staff Nurse Lester and, unpinning her apron, put on her cape and walked to the wing of the hospital which was the nurses' residence. Her room was small, little more than a cubicle, but she considered herself fortunate. The larger rooms were for three or four to share and she valued her privacy. There was worn linoleum on the floor, a narrow bed, a cupboard and a small chest of drawers. Flimsy floral-patterned curtains hung at the window, which looked out on to the car park and beyond that to fields.

All was dark out there now, except for an occasional dim light shining from a hospital window. The dining-room, however, was brightly lit and uncurtained. Helena watched members of the staff standing at the counter waiting to be served, or sitting at tables and chatting as they ate.

Suddenly she felt very alone, and wondered whether she would have been wiser to have taken a room in a boarding-house. It had been ideal at home, for their house was large and she could be alone or with her parents as the mood took her. When her father knew he was going to work in Kuwait he had suggested that she tried to get taken on at one of the many excellent hospitals there, but the idea had not appealed to Helena.

She leaned closer to the window. Was that glimpse of brown Mr Tracy's jacket? Impossible to tell from this distance. And no doubt he lived away from the hospital. It was strange that, although she had only seen him for a brief moment, she so clearly remembered his face. The half-closed eyes whose thick, curling lashes made it difficult to see whether the glint in them was of amusement or anger, and the mouth with its turned-down corners—was it suppressing a smile or showing disapproval? The rugged face was not, strictly speaking, handsome, but it was very attractive. She pictured his casual bearing and the way he walked with one hand thrust in his pocket.

Then she pulled herself together. How ridiculous! She was behaving just as Nurse Lester had predicted. Well, she decided determinedly, there will be no more foolish thoughts.

She moved briskly away from the window, pulled the curtains and undressed quickly. Soon she fell into a dreamless sleep, for it had been a long and tiring day.

CHAPTER TWO

IT WAS the sound of doors being slammed and drawers opened and shut which awoke Helena. For a moment she lay wondering where she was, then realisation came flooding back. She sat up in bed, reached for her watch and saw that if she wanted to have any breakfast she would have to get up straight away. Reluctantly she climbed out of bed and crossed over to the window.

Apart from the staff bay, the car park was empty. An ambulance, presumably on call, drove swiftly down the drive and out through the gates. She could see in the distance fields that were golden with a harvest of corn and somewhere nearby a bonfire sent a spiral of smoke into the blue sky. Helena could faintly hear the crackling twigs and smell the exciting tang. Overhead, seagulls soared and uttered raucous cries. Feeling that it was good to be alive on such a day, she washed and dressed and walked in the early morning freshness to the dining-room.

Here it could have been any hour of the day, for it was busy with the hum of conversation and clatter of dishes. She collected her breakfast and took her tray to the far end of the room, where she saw Nurse Coe sitting alone at a table for two.

'Hello, are you saving this place for someone?'

'No, sit yourself down. But I've almost finished and I've got to go back to my room for my pen. I'm always forgetting something.'

'It's such a beautiful morning! Aren't we lucky not to be ill in bed? I do feel sorry for the patients, especially those waiting in vain for their ops,' Helena said.

Nurse Coe raised her thin eyebrows. 'So you haven't heard? We're back to normal, the pickets have been called off. And the surgeons, bless 'em, can carve away to their hearts' content!'

'Thank goodness for that. What a relief for everybody!'

Her relief was echoed in the ward. There was a festive air as patients called to each other and joked and laughed as if they were going to a theatre to see a popular musical instead of being operated upon. Sister Bell was back on duty and the only person not pleased about that was Staff Nurse Lester, who had enjoyed her temporary authority.

'Good-morning, Nurse Chamberlain, are you settling in all right?' Sister Bell asked. She looked very neat and attractive in her darker shade of green dress with its small shoulder cape, and her more elaborate cap.

'Yes, thank you, Sister. I am glad you are better,' Helena said meekly.

'Thank you, Nurse, and I am glad to be better too, especially as today will be busy now that the go-slow is over. Mr Tracy will be coming in to speak to his patients and to reassure them as he always does before they go to theatre. So make sure the bedpans have been dealt with and the beds straight-

ened. He will be coming early.' She dismissed
Helena with a nod.

Despite her resolve to banish the surgeon from
her thoughts, Helena felt a quiver of anticipation at
the prospect of seeing him again. But the feeling
was momentary, for she had no time to dwell on
such matters. There were twelve beds to be made
with fresh draw-sheets and pillowcases. Helena and
Nurse Jelbart worked together, lifting patients who
were unable to raise themselves, and treating long-
stay patients to prevent bedsores by rubbing in
cream at their pressure points.

Helena checked that the patients who were to
have surgery were wearing their name-tags on their
wrists and that the site of their operation was
clearly and correctly marked on their bodies. Drips
were replaced and checked and any moment
now Staff Nurse Lester would return from her
meal break so that they could do the medicine
round.

There was a stir by the ward doors and a hush
descended on nearby patients. Mr Tracy, accompanied by Sister Bell, had arrived.

All heads turned towards them expectantly and
books and magazines were laid aside. At the
London hospital all the doctors had worn formal
suits when on duty, and Helena was surprised to
see that Mr Tracy was wearing his brown jacket.
His green tie was a bit askew, as if he had tied
it without glancing in a mirror. He seemed to
radiate colour and warmth and was like a ray of
sunshine in the drab ward. He walked slowly and
Sister Bell tapped beside him on higher heels than

were usually seen in the wards, her chest thrust forward importantly like a robin's.

They went first to the beds of the patients on whom he had already operated. He looked at the wall charts and then at the patients' notes before asking them if they had any problems. He listened carefully and sympathetically, had the bed curtains drawn so that he could examine their wounds to make sure they were healing satisfactorily, said a few cheery words and left them feeling satisfied that all was well with them. Having completed that round they began on those patients on whom he would be operating later in the day.

'Good-morning, Mrs Tonkin,' he said to a grey-haired, pale-faced woman. 'Has the hernia been causing you much trouble?'

She looked at him with eyes like a whipped spaniel. 'It has a bit, Doctor. It seems such a long time I've been waiting, it should have been over and done with a fortnight ago . . .' Her voice trailed away.

He laid his hand on hers. 'I know, Mrs Tonkin, it has been very trying for you and you have been very patient. But we will soon deal with it now. By next week you will feel a new woman.'

'Bless you, Doctor, and thank you.'

'I'll see you later,' he replied and raised his thumb encouragingly as he proceeded to his next patient.

'Hello, Miss Phillips, so today's the day!'

'Thank goodness for that, Doctor.'

'Yes. As you know, we had hoped that we would not need to operate. Ulcers will sometimes disappear with medication, but yours is an awkward customer apparently, so we will get rid of it once and for all.'

'And I'm glad about that. With medicines I'd always feel it might flare up again, and believe me I've had quite enough of that.'

'Yes, I'm sure you have.' He gave her a friendly smile. 'See you later.'

He stopped next at Mrs Penfold's bed. 'Hello, good-morning Mrs Penfold. You are looking very bright-eyed and bushy-tailed. Have you won the pools?'

She beamed happily. 'No, I don't want to win the pools, I just want my operation!'

He raised an eyebrow. 'I wish my patients were always so eager for my attention.'

'If anyone had told me before I came in here that I would be longing to have my operation I would have thought they were mad. But I am! It was the waiting, you see, it was awful. I'm so glad the strike is over.'

'So are we all, so are we all.' He sat casually on the edge of her bed, a thing which no surgeon, or anyone at all would have dared to do at St Ann's. 'But it will soon be over now, you are second on my list. I visualise that this is going to be a straightfor-ward operation, Mrs Penfold, but it is only to be expected that you will experience a certain amount of discomfort when you come around from the anaesthetic. This is usual and we will be able to give you something to ease it. And I am sure that after a day or two you will be feeling a lot better than you have done in years.'

'Thank you, Doctor. I feel quite safe to be in your hands. I know you will do your best for me.' She looked up at him devotedly.

He gave a boyish, embarrassed smile. 'Thank you. So you are quite happy about everything? Is there anything at all that you would like to ask me?'

She shook her head. 'No, thank you. I feel quite contented and not at all nervous, like I was yesterday. I think being allowed breakfast was good, it has made me feel stronger, better able to cope.'

If a bomb had exploded in the ward the sense of shock could not have been greater. It was as if everybody and everything in the vicinity was momentarily petrified. Then Sister Bell's pink and white cheeks flushed scarlet and her nostrils flared.

'What was that you said, Mrs Penfold?' she asked, aghast.

The smile left Mrs Penfold's face. 'I—I said I felt able to cope, Sister.'

'You said you were allowed breakfast?' Sister Bell persisted.

'Yes—it was brought to me—I—' she faltered.

'But you knew . . .' Sister Bell glanced quickly up at the wall behind her bed. 'What has happened to the "nil by mouth" notice?'

Mrs Penfold turned and squinted up. 'Isn't it there? Well I was moved, you see. I had been down there in the corner bed but I was moved because of Mrs Cooper needing attention during the night.'

Mr Tracy rose to his feet. His amiability had vanished as if it had never been.

'Who moved you here?' Sister Bell asked quietly.

'The—the new nurse—I forget her name. And—and Nurse Jelbart.'

Sister Bell searched the ward until her eyes alighted on Helena.

'Nurse Chamberlain,' she called sharply.

Helena hurried across to her. 'Yes, Sister?'

'Where is the "nil by mouth" notice for this patient?'

Helena looked at the blank wall and her face went ashen. Her blue eyes darkened in dismay as she looked down the ward to where the notice still hung over the wrong bed. How *could* she have forgotten to move it! She shook her head wordlessly.

Sister Bell gave her a black, withering look before turning to Mrs Penfold. 'You knew that you were not allowed anything to eat or drink before an operation. You must have been told that,' she said sternly.

Mrs Penfold's eyes clouded. 'Yes I was, and I didn't have anything to eat all day yesterday, so when they brought me breakfast I thought it must be all right. And of course, I didn't know for sure that I was going to have my operation. Nobody said anything.'

Mr Tracy laid his hand on her shoulder. 'I am very sorry indeed that there has been this mix-up, because I am afraid that it means you will not be operated on today. I'll do it tomorrow, I promise you.'

Tears sprang to her eyes as she plucked at the bedcover. 'Oh please, Mr Tracy, can't you do it today? I didn't eat a lot—and I don't mind if I'm sick afterwards—I'll put up with that.'

He shook his head firmly but regretfully. 'I am really sorry for this postponement, but it is completely out of the question for the operation to proceed.'

'Nurse Chamberlain, please go to my office immediately.' Sister Bell's voice was as hard and cold as ice-cubes rattling in a tumbler.

With feet like heavy weights hung on elastic, Helena left the ward, aware that all eyes were on her but caring most that Mr Tracy was a witness to her mortification.

Sister Bell's office looked bleak and impersonal. The only chair was behind the large, light wooden desk with a mass of paperwork set on it in neat piles. Charts and rotas were pinned to the walls and the only frivolous note was provided by a number of pot-plants which stood on the window sill. Helena dared not sit on Sister Bell's chair so she leaned against the wall, for her legs felt almost too weak to hold her.

She dreaded the forthcoming interview. She knew the vital importance of the 'nil by mouth' rule, it had been dinned into every student from the very start of training, and she would never know how she had come to overlook its transfer. She had checked name-tags and that the operation site was clearly marked, so why, oh why had she not checked that the notice was in its correct place? Night staff who served breakfast were in no way to blame, for they had nothing else to go by . . .

Not the least of her distress was for Mrs Penfold herself, for her disappointment and frustration at the further delay. Helena was thankful from the bottom of her heart that Mrs Penfold had mentioned the fact that she had eaten, for had she not done so the result could have been catastrophic.

At the sound of approaching footsteps her heart began a steady thump of apprehension. She straightened up and glanced fearfully towards the door. To her utter dismay she saw that Sister Bell was not alone—but was accompanied by Mr Tracy.

With a flurry of starched apron Sister went to her desk like an indignant bird. Her nose wore a pinched look and her mouth was no bigger than a buttonhole. Mr Tracy stood beside her, large and craggy. The lines on his face were set deeply, his mouth was turned down, his eyes furiously angry.

Everything inside Helena seemed to slither downwards and her knees trembled. She looked desperately from one to the other of them and ran her tongue over her dry lips.

'Nurse—?' The doctor looked at Sister Bell for confirmation of her name.

'Chamberlain. Nurse Chamberlain, sir.'

He turned to Helena. 'Nurse Chamberlain, in my many years in hospital work I have not come across more culpable behaviour.' He paused, and his eyes seemed to pierce hers. After a moment he continued, 'Have you any idea of the seriousness of your conduct?' His voice was harsh and resonant.

Her eyes were wide and tragic. 'Oh yes, sir, I have and I regret it very much.'

He frowned and Helena saw that the lines around his eyes had not only been caused by laughter. 'Regret it? Of course you regret it. We all regret it, and nobody more so than the patient herself. You can count yourself extremely fortunate that she mentioned the fact that she had eaten, because she only did so inadvertently.'

'I know, sir,' she whispered.

'And I trust that you also know that we could have had a death on our hands and *I*—not you—but *I* would have been held responsible! That is something I have no wish to contemplate.'

Helena lowered her gaze against the leashed-in anger behind his self-control, the blaze in his eyes. 'I—I'm sorry, sir.'

He thrust a hand in his trouser pocket. 'How long have you been working here?' he asked abruptly.

'N—nearly a week, sir.'

His eyebrows shot up. 'Nearly a week.' He turned to Sister Bell. 'Who was in charge at the time, Sister?'

'Staff Nurse Lester was in charge as I was away sick, sir.'

'Then she is responsible, is she not?'

Helena remembered how busy they had been and that Nurse Lester had been in here answering telephone calls.

'I was responsible for the change-over, Sister. Nurse Lester was called away,' she admitted hastily.

'Mr Tracy did not address you, Nurse. Kindly do not speak unless you are spoken to,' Sister Bell snapped. She turned to the doctor and said in quite a different tone of voice, 'Staff had her hands full with just a newcomer and a junior on the ward with her. But yes, she is ultimately responsible. Do you wish me to send for her, sir?'

He stared hard at Helena, his eyes boring into her as if they would dig out everything in her mind. After a moment's consideration he said, 'No, I'll leave her to you. As for you, Nurse, I cannot find words to express my anger. Where were you trained?'

She tried to speak but no sound would come. She tried again.

'At St Ann's. In London, sir.'

'St Ann's? And what a disgraceful ambassador for a splendid hospital you have proved to be! What do you imagine the very excellent sister tutor there would have to say about your behaviour?'

He sounded so angry that to her dismay Helena felt the sting of tears in her eyes. She breathed deeply and prayed silently that the tears would not fall.

'Well?' he demanded.

She stood quite still, unable to make the slightest movement or sound in case her prayer was not answered.

'You must understand that we are proud of Trelawny Hospital and our reputation. If you entertain any hope of staying on here you had better not be involved in any more such incidents, or you will most certainly be required to leave. We will not want you here.'

Helena managed to whisper, 'Yes, sir.'

He stared at her for a moment longer, his eyes as grey as pewter. Then he turned to Sister Bell.

'Please see that this reprimand is written up in

Nurse Chamberlain's report for administration.'

Sister Bell jotted something down on her pad. 'Yes sir, I will do that.'

Some of the anger seemed to leave him and he appeared more relaxed.

'I think that is all. I must get on, I have lost too much time as it is.' He turned to Helena. 'And you, Nurse, I suggest you go to our patient and offer your apologies.'

'Yes, sir,' she was able to murmur.

She looked across at Sister Bell who nodded briefly. 'You may go now.'

The doctor was already at the door and held it open for her. Outside he paused as if he intended saying something else and she held her breath in fearful anticipation. His face was just a blur for her eyes were misty with unshed tears.

To break the silence she began, 'I—I am desperately sorry—' then could say no more.

Something stirred in his eyes. It was as if the hardness was thawing and being replaced by a flicker of something kinder, more gentle. He laid his hand on her shoulder.

'Don't cry, my dear, we all make mistakes at some time. We are all human beings,' he said softly.

Her heart seemed to swell. Her body, where he was touching her, felt alive, vibrant. But she could not speak. He waited a moment for her to make some reply, but when none was forthcoming he strode away. Helena made a dash for the kitchen. Then tears streamed down her cheeks.

She knew that she deserved every censorious

word he had said, and more. Nobody could condemn her more than she did herself. If only it had not happened, if only she had not appeared in such a bad light to Mr Tracy of all people. He had been justifiably angry, and she understood that. What she did not understand was why he had suddenly been so kind. That had affected her more than his anger and made her realise just why he was so adored by staff and patients alike. Why, oh why had she been unable to speak, so that it looked as if she was sulking?

When her tears were spent she braced herself for her return to the ward. She splashed her face with cold water, blew her nose and straightened her cap.

The curtains had been drawn around Mrs Penfold's bed and Helena parted them reluctantly. The patient was lying on her back, staring up at the ceiling with a look of blank despair. Helena took hold of her hands, fearing that she might, however, drag them away.

'What can I say?' Helena asked miserably.

'It's no good saying anything, Nurse. Mr Tracy won't operate today, that's certain,' she sighed.

'I'll never know how I came to forget that notice. I—I can't understand it.' Helena shook her head.

Mrs Penfold moved her eyes so that she could look at Helena.

'It wasn't all your fault, Nurse, I was as much to blame.'

'Oh you weren't, it isn't your responsibility at all,' Helena replied hastily.

'No, I know it isn't my responsibility but I shouldn't have eaten that breakfast, I should have thought to question it. The fact is, I wanted that first cup of tea so badly and when nobody said anything I ate my breakfast when it was brought to me.'

'I understand and I know just how you felt. But thank goodness you told Mr Tracy, or it could have been very serious,' Helena murmured.

'I wished afterwards that I hadn't said anything because I knew that I'd got you into trouble—and I wouldn't have done that for the world, you've been so kind to me. I do hope they weren't too hard on you.'

Helena shook her head. 'No more than I deserved.'

Mrs Penfold pushed herself to a sitting position. 'Well, that's that, I'm not going to do myself or anyone else any good, lying here moping. Tomorrow will come in its own good time and in the meantime I'm going to enjoy whatever food comes my way. Here, Nurse, have one of these.' She felt in her locker and brought out a tin of peppermints.

'Mrs Penfold, you really shouldn't—'

Popping one into her mouth before Helena could stop her, she gave a naughty smile. 'It's too late for you to do anything about it now.'

Helena shook her head. 'One way or another you're going to be the death of me. Whatever would Sister Bell say?'

'Who cares? I'm going to enjoy myself today to take my mind off . . .' Her voice trailed away and the smile left her face. 'You run away, Nurse, I know you've got your work to do. I'll be all right.'

Helena drew back the curtains. 'I'm sorry, Mrs Penfold, but I have to open them.'

'That's all right, Nurse.' She raised her voice and called to the patient in the opposite bed, 'I'm the lucky one. I've got a day's reprieve!'

Sister Bell had given Mrs Tonkin her pre-med and was now standing by her bedside looking worried.

'Nurse Chamberlain,' she called over her shoulder.

Helena finished her observations of Mrs Cooper, entered her readings on her card, then hurried across the ward. 'Sister?'

Sister Bell moved away from the patient and said in an undertone, 'Mrs Tonkin is going for her hernia op and I want you to accompany her.' Already there was the sound of a rubber-wheeled trolley approaching. A porter stopped beside Sister Bell.

'Tonkin. Mrs Rose Tonkin,' he checked his list.

'That's right.' Sister again checked the patient's name-tag before helping to transfer her to the trolley.

As Helena walked beside it and into the lift, Mrs Tonkin looked at her with drowsy eyes.

'You will stay with me, won't you?'

'Yes, I will. Don't you worry, I'll be there,' Helena said.

They entered the reception area of the operating suite and Helena handed over the necessary forms to the theatre nurse there. As they waited for the anaesthetist to appear, Mr Tracy walked into the room, obviously on his way to scrub up for the operation.

His eyes alighted on Helena. 'What are you doing here, Nurse?'

'I accompanied Mrs Tonkin,' she said coolly. 'On Sister Bell's instructions.'

He nodded briskly and disappeared into the ante-room to prepare. Soon the anaesthetist arrived and introduced himself, but Mrs Tonkin was already too sleepy to reply. When he gave her an injection in the back of her hand she obviously felt nothing and, completely unconscious, was wheeled away while Helena returned to the ward.

It was only an hour or so later that she was summoned to collect Mrs Tonkin from the recovery room. Mr Tracy was there, too, checking one of the patients he had just finished operating on. Helena tried to ignore him as she took details of Mrs Tonkin's post-operative care.

As she was leaving with her patient, she turned to have a final look around. At the same moment Mr Tracy glanced over his shoulder and their eyes met and held. Then Helena lowered hers and walked away.

But her thoughts remained behind with the man who watched her go.

CHAPTER THREE

HELENA SAT in the dining-room beside a window which looked out over fields to the sea, which was turbulent and grey and threw up fountains of spray. It had been a blustery night with typically Cornish gale force winds that had battered the windows until they rattled in their frames and stripped slates from roof-tops. Now it had subsided and everywhere looked fresh and clean, as if it had been well-washed.

It was a day to entice you out of doors, and as Helena thoughtfully buttered a slice of toast she looked forward to the few days leave due to her which she intended to spend with the aunt who lived in Stipplewick and who was the reason why she had chosen to work in Cornwall. The dining-room was half empty, so when a young doctor took his seat at her table with a pleasant 'Do you mind?' she looked at him in surprise.

His twinkling blue eyes were extremely self-confident and he spoke in a self-assured voice. 'So, where have you been all my life?'

Helena glanced at him coldly, despite the fact that he was good-looking in an obvious way. He had good features and a small flaxen moustache which was the colour of his hair. Surely he could have thought up a more original way to introduce himself!

'I hope you appreciated my approach?' With a pleasant smile he reached for the sugar and stirred some into his coffee.

'No, I can't say that I did. To be truthful, I felt you could have done better.'

'Like telling you my name?'

Helena believed she knew who he was. 'Don't tell me, let me guess.' She frowned in pretended concentration. 'Could it be that your name, sir, is Bill?' She opened her eyes wide in question.

He placed a hand theatrically on his heart. 'She knows me! How come that you guessed aright, sweet damsel? In faith my name is William Wood.'

A smile came into her eyes. 'Yes, indeed. I heard, from all and sundry, that Bill *would* if he got the chance. Is that true?'

He looked delighted. 'Completely true. I will at any time. So where the place?'

She gave him a sideways glance. 'Not upon the heath, that's for sure.'

She noticed his gold identity bracelet and the gold chain with some bauble on it which hung around his neck. Never in a million years could she imagine Mr Tracy so bedecked. They were two doctors, roughly in the same age group, although Bill was probably a few years younger, both good-looking—yet totally different.

Everything about Bill, his dress, his speech, his manner, was meant to impress; whereas Mr Tracy appeared to be totally indifferent to the effect he had on people. Although it was surely not possible that he could be unaware of his own attraction . . .

Helena frowned, annoyed with herself. Why, for heaven's sake, did thoughts of Mr Tracy keep intruding when she had determined to banish him from her mind? In the course of her work she had to see him frequently, but surely she should have control over her thoughts?

Bill was chatting to her, asking her questions about herself to which she was replying automatically. She pulled herself together and gave him her attention.

'When you have time off let me know, and I'll try to arrange mine to match. There are lots of places and things I could show you, that you ought to see.' He looked at her with flattering intensity.

'I'll bet there are,' she said, looking at him through narrowed eyes. 'But you have to remember that you are not talking to a naive Cornish girl. You see before you a hard-bitten Londoner who has frequently met your sort before.'

'You know how to wound a chap,' he said reproachfully. Then he grinned. 'So you are hard-to-get Helena.'

She looked at him in surprise. 'I didn't tell you my name.'

He laughed. 'In this hospital nothing is secret, or indeed sacred. When a new nurse arrives we make strategic enquiries, find out all about her. At least, *I* do, because I am very fond of nurses and, heaven be praised, they seem to be fond of me.'

'You probably have no competition,' she murmured.

'That is where you are mistaken. It seems that I

have a rival and goodness knows why, because he has none of my charm. He is older for a start, aloof, has a sharp tongue in his head and is not all that keen on the ladies. Yet for some obscure reason women of all shapes and sizes fall for him. Which just goes to show how irrational they are.'

Helen's thoughts flew to Mr Tracy. 'So who is this old Casanova?'

'Nobody that you need bother your pretty head about. He's way high-up—my boss in fact—and he would never condescend to have dealings with anyone below the rank of sister.'

Helena's heart shuddered. 'Sister Bell for example?'

'Ah! So you do know about him. Don't tell me that you've already fallen for him?' He looked at her reproachfully.

'Of course not, I know my lowly place. I had to accompany a patient with a dicky heart who he was operating on, so I crawled in on my hands and knees,' Helena said as casually as she could.

He looked at her with mischievous eyes. 'I heard on the grape-vine that some foolish little nurse let a patient have brekkers before her op! My boss was livid and rumour has it that he can't wait to have her chucked out. I wouldn't be in her shoes.'

Helena's mouth went dry. She felt certain that Bill knew that she was the culprit and was teasing her. But was what he said about Mr Tracy true? Was he determined to get her dismissed?

'Can—can he do that?' she faltered.

But Bill's attention had wandered and, looking for the cause of his distraction, she saw Coe approaching, carrying a tray. Her face was flushed and unusually bright. She obviously had eyes for nobody but Bill.

Bill stood up to fetch her a chair. 'Here she is, the girl of my dreams.'

Helena glanced at her watch. 'Don't think the sight of you has driven me away, Coe,' she smiled, 'but I'm due back right now.'

She stopped at the ward kitchen to collect the flowers that had been brought from the ward over-night, and took them back to the patients. Flowers, she often thought, were a mixed blessing. They brightened up the ward and no doubt it cheered the patients to think that loved ones had thought of them, but they created a lot of extra work and took up valuable space on locker tops.

Today was not an operating day but Mr Tracy would be making his usual round. Mrs Penfold had now had her operation and was making good progress. Mrs Tonkin, on the other hand, was not doing so well, her fluctuating pulse rate was giving rise to anxiety and she needed careful watching.

A Mrs Plumley had been admitted the previous day and was understandably nervous. Apparently everything had happened quickly. She was drying herself after a bath when she felt a lump in her breast. She had spent the day alternately thinking it was just an enlarged muscle and then that it was cancer. She thrust that frightening thought aside, telling herself that if it was anything serious she would be in pain. But after a sleepless night she went to see her doctor. He examined her and the following day she had come to the hospital for X-rays. And then she was admitted.

She was a comparatively wealthy widow in her fifties and firmly believed that she should have a private room.

'We don't have private rooms in Trelawny, Mrs Plumley,' Sister Bell said.

'I believe you have side rooms. I would like one of those.'

Sister Bell eyed her sternly. 'We use the side rooms at our own discretion,' she said in a no-nonsense voice.

'And what does that mean?' the patient asked imperiously.

'It means that when and if we consider it would be beneficial for a patient to be on her own for some good reason, we put her in there. You do not come into that category.' Sister walked smartly away, her apron crackling with displeasure.

'It isn't as if I'm asking for it for free, I am quite willing to pay,' Mrs Plumley said peevishly to Helena.

'Nobody pays for them, Mrs Plumley. Actually, they are not used very often, but if a nurse was taken ill she would go in one because it would be better for her to be away from the patients.'

'I loathe the idea of being in a public ward with all these . . . these people. Just being in here is enough to make me ill,' the woman grumbled, looking around her with distaste.

'I'm sorry, but there is nothing I can do about it. And you will find that all the patients are very nice when you get to know them.'

'You may think so.' Mrs Plumley gave her an unfriendly look.

'Nurse! Nurse!' a plaintive voice cried urgently.

'Yes, Miss Truelove?' Helena crossed the ward to where an elderly lady was holding the bedclothes away from her. A bottle of orange squash rolled on the bed.

'The stopper came off in my hand and it's all over the place. I'm all sticky. I'm sorry, dearie, but it's my hands, they're that shaky.'

Helena picked up the bottle and replaced the top. Then she examined the bed-linen to see what damage had been caused.

'We'll need to change all this, won't we?' she said, and drew the curtains.

'Oh, I am sorry, it's so sticky and it seems to have got over everything!'

'Well not to worry, we'll soon get you changed.'

As she was passing Mrs Tonkin's bed she glanced at her automatically, then looked again and hurried to her side. She saw the ashen face and felt for her pulse. Then she raced to Sister Bell's office.

'Cardiac arrest, Sister. Mrs Tonkin,' she gasped.

Sister Bell was out of her office even as she spoke. 'Call the cardiac arrest unit, Nurse.' She began the cardiac re-start routine, so ingrained into every nurse.

Helena grabbed the telephone and dialled, just as Mr Tracy was walking casually along the corridor towards the ward to do his round.

'Cardiac arrest, Mr Tracy!' she cried urgently.

He sped past her in a flash, followed soon afterwards by the team. Helena stayed where she was, feeling shaken and helpless. She would only be in the way of the experts if she returned to the bedside, so she took some deep breaths to steady her shaking limbs then continued on her way to fetch the clean linen and hot water.

She needed to sponge Miss Truelove all over, replace her nightdress and strip the bed. When she had made the patient comfortable she washed down the bedside locker, then took the sticky fruit and washed it at the sink in the ward before replacing it.

'Nurse!' The calls came from all corners of the ward. It was as if the drama of the cardiac arrest had made the other patients nervous and they all needed attention of one kind or another.

Miss Truelove called her back. 'Nurse, dear, I'm so sorry to be such a nuisance but these clean sheets and nightdress are freezing cold and my feet are like ice. Do you think I could have a hot water bottle and—and a hot drink, please?' she whimpered.

'Of course.'

Helena hurried to the kitchen. These were such simple requests. It was natural for an old lady to want such comforts and Helena sympathised. Yet she knew that if other patients spotted her being given these little extras they too would demand them. Still, that was a nurse's life.

It was Mrs Plumley's ultra-refined voice that summoned her.

'Nurse,' she said as Helena was passing, 'these are not my flowers.' She pointed disdainfully at the vase of Michaelmas daisies on her locker top.

'Oh, aren't they? Well, never mind, I daresay you can have them. Let's wait until someone asks for them,' Helena said amiably.

'How dare you! I don't want someone else's half-dead flowers! I want my own hot-house blooms that I brought in with me yesterday. Oh, I have no doubt you have given them to one of your favourites, together with other little luxuries like hot milk and hot water bottles,' she said spitefully.

'No, Mrs Plumley I haven't done that deliberately. If you tell me what flowers you had I will try and find them for you.'

'You will not only try to find them, you *will* find them or buy me some more. And you can take these away!' She snatched the daisies with their wet, woody stems from the vase and threw them on to her bedcover. 'And I don't want to lie here in a wet bed or I will complain to the hospital board.' She moved her legs irritably so that the flowers fell to the floor.

Helena stooped to pick them up.

'And wipe the floor. I don't want my visitors sitting here in discomfort.'

'The wet floor and your wet bedcover are of your own making,' Helena said, trying unsuccessfully to control her temper.

Mrs Plumley's voice was menacing. 'How dare you speak to me like that!'

Helena heard someone approaching and looked up to see Mr Tracy. She flushed to the roots of her hair.

'Good-morning, Mrs Plumley,' he said in his resonant voice. 'I expect you are feeling a little on edge at the thought of the exploratory operation tomorrow, but believe me we are doing them all the time, so you don't need to worry.' He gave her a charming smile.

Helena remained on her knees, for she was afraid her legs might not support her if she attempted to stand up.

'Oh, Mr Tracy I wish your nurses were as caring as you are,' Mrs Plumley said, looking up at him from under heavily made-up lashes.

He wrinkled up his forehead. 'My nurses? Come now, I am very proud of my staff, Mrs Plumley. What could be kinder than for Nurse Chamberlain to pick up the flowers you have just thrown down?'

At that moment Helena felt she wanted to throw her arms around him in gratitude.

'She brought me these, these—*weeds*—quite deliberately, when she knew quite well that I had hot-house chrysanthemums! She and Sister seem determined that I shall be uncomfortable. No private room for me, oh no! They say they allocate them to the patients they choose, give me half-dead flowers . . .'

He interrupted her and said sternly, 'Now, Mrs Plumley, I cannot allow you to speak of my nurses in this way. If you do, you and I are going to fall out.'

He moved a short distance away from the bed and said loudly and clearly to Helena, 'Thank you very much, Nurse, for being so kind as to clear up for Mrs Plumley. I am sorry you had the extra work.' He looked straight into her eyes and for a moment it seemed as if they shared a secret.

Helena levered herself up, took the armful of flowers and hurried with them to the kitchen. She would never, ever, get over the wonderful feeling of hearing him stand up for her in the way he had!

She closed her eyes and stood by the sink in rapt memory, clasping the flowers to her breast, telling herself that she loved him . . . loved him. After a few minutes she came alive again and saw the greenish water dripping down her apron. With a smothered curse she hurried to the linen room to find a replacement. As she skidded round the corner she almost collided with someone who steadied her with firm hands.

'Oh I'm sorry,' she said. Then wished that she could sink through the floor.

'You *are* after my blood, aren't you, Nurse?' Mr Tracy said mildly.

'I'm sorry,' she said again, looking away from the cool grey eyes. She was unable to pass him, not only because his large body blocked her path, but because his hands were still gripping her arms.

'And don't forget that I am after yours, Nurse.'

'After mine?' Her eyes flew open. That was what Bill had implied!

'Yes, Nurse. I warned you before about your carelessness. It may only be the wrong flowers today—or a soiled apron.' He glanced down at it. 'Tomorrow it could be something far more serious. Do you get my meaning?'

She hung her head. 'Yes, sir,' she murmured.

'Good.' He laid a lean forefinger under her chin and tilted up her face to look into his.

At the unfathomable expression in his eyes and his proximity she felt her body grow weak and a shiver passed through her.

'So no more mistakes, eh, Nurse?'

'No, sir,' she breathed.

'Good. It would be too bad if we had to part company so soon in your career, don't you agree? But we cannot employ nurses who are irresponsible.'

He took his hand from her chin and stepped aside, then continued on his way along the corridor.

Helena stood still, her heart pounding. What power he had to twist her feelings as if he was wringing out a cloth. Why did he have such an effect on her? Not one of the many doctors at St Ann's had caused her a moment's concern, yet they were clever, dedicated men and, thinking back, some of them were young and quite good-looking. But she had seldom come into contact with them, it was as if they lived in a world apart. Here, because it was so much smaller, she was meeting Mr Tracy all the time.

A frightening thought wormed itself into her mind. Surely she wasn't falling in love with him? If asked, she would strenuously deny it. And yet—to feel weak at the thought of him, to continually visualise his large, casual figure and his lined face, which looked as if he was smiling when he wasn't; to seem to hear his cultured, resonant voice when he was nowhere near and to long with all her heart to feel his arms around her—what was that if it was not love?

Even so, she hated the fact that he could and did look at her so coldly when she felt so warm towards him. He could say such cruel, shaming things and imply that her future career at the hospital lay in his hands. But most of all she hated the thought that he might be in love with Sister Bell.

Love—hate—what was it that she felt for him? More important, did it make a scrap of difference? He would not care one way or the other, of that she was certain.

She made her way slowly back to the ward. Sister Bell stopped her.

'Mrs Tonkin has responded to treatment, Nurse, but has been sent to intensive care so that she can be under constant surveillance.' She was about to walk away, then paused. 'Are you having trouble with Mrs Plumley?'

'Yes, Sister, she is being rather difficult. But she must be very worried. I know I would be.'

'To be worried is one thing. To be rude to us is quite another. If all is found to be well tomorrow she should be discharged in a day or so,' Sister said reassuringly.

'And if it isn't?' Helena asked.

'If it isn't, I might find it in my heart to be more

sympathetic towards her,' the senior nurse replied.

'Yes, Sister. It isn't always easy, is it?'

Sister Bell smiled. 'Let's face it, we are only human. In what other walk of life would people think they had the right to treat us the way some of our patients do?'

'That's true. But on the other hand, most of them are very grateful and that makes up for it, doesn't it, Sister?' Helena said cheerfully.

'Nurse!' Sister's voice changed dramatically. 'Where *have* you been? You look as if you've been in a pigsty in that apron. Just look at it!'

'Oh heavens! I forgot to change it,' Helena admitted, looking down at the green stains. 'I'm sorry, Sister, I'll do it right away.'

Sister Bell gave a sigh. 'I don't know what we are going to do about you, Nurse. It's just one mistake after another, isn't it? And you had better find Mrs Plumley's precious flowers or there will be more trouble.'

Helena found the chrysanthemums on Mrs Hugh's locker. Five beautiful, mop-headed blooms in palest yellow. No wonder Mrs Plumley had been so annoyed by their disappearance.

'Shouldn't you have Michaelmas daisies, Mrs Hugh?' she asked.

A shadow fell over the old lady's face. 'Yes, Nurse, I suppose so. But these are so beautiful. Thank you for putting them there. I've just loved looking at them.'

Helena smiled sympathetically. 'I'm sorry, but I'm afraid their time with you is up. They must go back to their rightful owner. Still, having them was nice while it lasted, wasn't it?'

'Whose are they, then?' Mrs Hugh asked.

'They belong to Mrs Plumley,' Helena said coolly.

Mrs Hugh looked enviously at the woman wearing the expensive lace-bordered satin bedjacket and sniffed. 'Of course, they would be hers. Has she missed them?'

'Of course she has. Wouldn't you have done?'

'Yes, I would that! Anyhow, my neighbour will be coming to visit me and she would feel hurt if her Michaelmas daisies weren't here on my locker. Though they grow like weeds in her garden—and in mine!' She gave a conspiratorial laugh.

Helena carried the flowers across to Mrs Plumley. 'Here you are, back with you all safe and sound. They are really beautiful, no wonder you didn't want to lose them.'

Mrs Plumley gave Helena a sidelong glance. 'I am sorry for being so short-tempered earlier on, I know it was rude and unkind of me, but the truth is I'm worried to death.' Her voice trailed away.

'Of course you are, Mrs Plumley, anyone would be. But let's keep our fingers crossed that all will be well. A lot of these lumps prove to be benign, you know.'

'So they tell me. How long will it be before they know for sure?'

'I think they know straight away. They take out the lump and rush it across to the lab for tests. At least, that is what they did at my London hospital. I haven't been here long enough to know if it's the same here.'

'And—and when they know?'

'I believe that if they find it is malignant they complete the operation then and there.'

'You mean—you mean they might take off my breast tomorrow?' Mrs Plumley looked horrified.

'That saves a second operation, you see—it is better done immediately. But you mustn't look on the black side, it could as easily be an ordinary cyst. And you have done all you could, you wasted no time in seeing your doctor and they admitted you straight away. That is the most anyone can do.'

Mrs Plumley nodded and stared into space. 'I realise that I am just a statistic, one of many women facing the same thing. I tell myself that, but it doesn't make it any easier. I suppose everyone thinks it can only happen to someone else.'

Helena laid a comforting hand on her shoulder, unable to think of any useful reply. Indeed, Mrs Plumley did not seem to expect a reply, she was merely voicing her thoughts. As Helena was going off duty Sister Bell called her back.

'I have been doing the duty rosters, Nurse. Normally you would be having four days off after working ten days, but as I am short-staffed on Friday I shall have to split those four days and give you Thursday off, and then the weekend starting Saturday. Will that be all right?'

The question was rhetorical. Sister Bell expected no answer and certainly no objection. So Helena said the only thing possible.

'Yes, that will be quite all right, thank you, Sister.' But her heart was heavy with disappointment.

CHAPTER FOUR

THE DINING-ROOM on this Wednesday night was noisy with the buzz of conversation, which had to be loud to be heard over the clatter of plates and cutlery and the rattle of trays as nurses and doctors queued for their evening meal.

'Would you credit it, Collins?' Helena sighed.

'Yes, love, I'd believe anything you told me. What especially on this occasion?'

'I've got tomorrow off, then I'm on duty on Friday and then I've got the weekend off. What a waste of one lovely day! I don't know what to do with it. Or this,' Helena added as she ate the cottage pie and wondered in how many ways minced meat could be permutated.

'It sounds like the clever manoeuvring of Sister Bell.'

'That's right. Don't tell me she makes a habit of it?'

'Let's say it is not unusual,' Collins raised a knowing eyebrow.

Helena groaned. 'You're a great comfort!'

'I'm just putting you in the picture so that you don't think this is a unique experience.'

'If only I had a car I could drive over to my aunt. She lives in Stipplewick,' Helena mused.

'Crumbs, you do want to see life! If I had a car I'd hope to do something more exciting with it.'

'Such as what?'

Collins shrugged. 'Stipplewick isn't far, is it? Why don't you go by bus?'

'I did think of that, but according to the timetable I would have to take two buses and surprise, surprise, they don't connect up. So I'd spend half the day waiting at the bus-stop and my poor old legs don't fancy that. I don't really like cottage pie even when it's nice.' She ate another mouthful, then pushed her plate aside.

'I second both those remarks. Why not give Stipplewick a miss and go somewhere like Helston or St Ives or wherever there is a fairly good service?'

'What do I do when I get there?' Helena asked plaintively.

'I don't know. Walk around the shops, have a spot of lunch—maybe some cottage pie if you're lucky,' Collins said with a grin.

'On my own? That's not much fun.'

'True, but it's more or less the story of my life.'

Helena's eyes brightened. 'Oh! Come to think of it, Bill Wood offered to show me round if we happened to be off duty at the same time. I suppose I could get on to him to see if he is free.' She looked around the dining-room hopefully.

'Uh-huh!' Collins gave her a warning shake of the head. 'Carefully does it, my girl. Do you want your eyes scratched out?'

'Not particularly. Why? Do I stand a chance of that?'

'Not 'arf you don't!'

'Who would do this dastardly deed?'

'Any one of us,' Collins said cheerfully.

Helena grinned. 'I'll risk it. Anything is better than staying in and washing my hair.'

'Especially as it doesn't need doing, it always looks nice. It's a nice shade of brown. Do you use a rinse?'

'No, of course I don't, it's natural mouse! Now, if I wanted to colour it I'd go the whole hog and make it yellow—only I don't think it would suit me. What I'd really love to have is very blonde, dead-straight hair.'

'Yes, I like that look too, only it doesn't look all that good under a cap. Penny Barker in casualty has got really long hair and she is forever shedding hairpins. I'd choose that rich copper colour.'

'So, what's stopping you?' Helena enquired.

'Having to go to the hairdresser every week or so.'

'I'd hate that.'

'Me too. Especially when it came to paying for it,' Collins giggled.

'Mmm.' They were silent for a few moments as they tackled their plum crumble.

Then Collins said, 'Can you ride a bike?'

'Oh yes,' Helena said thoughtfully. 'That's an idea! I wonder if I could hire one from somewhere?'

'I don't know. But Coe has got one.'

Helena's eyes lit up hopefully. 'Do you suppose she would lend it to me?'

Collins shrugged. 'She probably would if it would keep your sticky paws off Bill.'

'Bill? Why? Is she especially keen on him?'

'Yes. But then, most of us are. You must admit, he's very dishy.'

'I don't know. I should think he was good fun to be with. You talk a lot about him being attractive, but I thought Mr Tracy was supposed to be everyone's pin-up?' Helena protested.

'Well, he is of course, there's no disputing that. But Bill is more or less within our reach and Mr Tracy isn't.'

'Well I can't imagine Bill getting serious about anyone, really.'

'No, but it isn't impossible,' Collins insisted.

'I'll have a word with Coe about her bike. Thanks for telling me.'

'Mind you, it's only an old bone-shaker. I should think it was a throw-out from a museum. I can't really recommend it.' Nurse Collins' eyes slid sideways. 'And here is your alternative!'

Bill, looking attractive in his white coat with a stethoscope tucked in the pocket, was approaching their table with a cup of coffee.

He smiled at them both. 'I've just nipped out for a crafty cup. Is there room for a very nice, slim young doctor at this table? Who would like the privilege of sitting on my knee?'

Helena jumped up. 'Sorry, you're out of luck, I'm on my way. You can take my place.'

Bill put his cup down and stood looking at her. 'Helena, my pet, we haven't fixed that date yet. You are still playing hard to get!'

Helena and Collins exchanged a smile. 'So I am! But just keep on trying, and who knows? One of these days—maybe sooner than you think—oh excuse me, I've just seen Coe.'

Helena threaded her way around the tables until she reached Coe, who was queuing at the counter. 'Hello and goodbye, I'm just going. But Collins is over there—near the far end—and Bill is there too.'

Coe's round brown eyes lit up as she looked in the direction that Helena was pointing. 'Thanks for telling me.'

'I was hoping to see you. Collins said you had a bike and I wondered if I could borrow it tomorrow?'

'Tomorrow? Why, have you got the day off?'

'Yes, just the one. I wanted to go to Stipplewick but the buses are hopeless.'

'Stipplewick? How far is that?'

'I'm not sure. About five miles I should think. Too far to walk.'

'And a heck of a way on my old bike! But you're welcome to borrow it—rather you than me,' Coe laughed.

Helena squeezed her arm. 'You're a pal. Good luck with Bill.'

The next morning Helena was awake early. The sky was clear and blue and there was a crisp autumnal tang in the air. She had breakfast in the dining-room and enjoyed the sausage and bacon far more, knowing that she had a journey ahead of her, than if she had to spend the day on the ward.

Coe had been speaking the truth when she said her bicycle was old-fashioned. It was so tall that

Helena felt she needed a step-ladder to reach the saddle, but she set off in high spirits to the sound of cheers from doctors and nurses who were going on duty. After a while she began to think that it might have been as quick to walk the distance, for some of the hills were so steep that she had to dismount and push the bike. But she had the compensation of free-wheeling down the other side.

Her Aunt Norah had been delighted when Helena had telephoned to ask if she might come for the day. She had spent most of her working life in Stipplewick after training at St Ann's. She had come to Cornwall as a district nurse and midwife and had only recently retired. Although Stipplewick was a fair-sized village she maintained that she knew practically all the inhabitants. Indeed, she went further and said she had brought a large number of them into the world! Helena, who had spent numerous holidays with her over the years, found it both amusing and embarrassing to be with her when she addressed middle-aged men and women by their christian names and spoke to them as if they were still at infant school.

Aunt Norah had one glaring fault. It was her overwhelming desire to be a matchmaker. She would blissfully point out married couples who owed their marital state to her conniving and she boasted proudly that it was through her manoeuvring that Helena's mother had met and married Thomas Chamberlain. That had proved to be an outstanding success and for the last few years she had eyed Helena consideringly and trotted out men of all types whenever she came to stay.

Indeed, it was memories of these embarrassing occasions that had almost made Helena doubt the wisdom of visiting her. Middle-aged men, young ones, thin or stout, single or—well she had never actually produced any married men because that would have been against her principles—but even those mildly committed had been fair game. All these had been invited to the house on some pretext and urged to stay for a meal. Not that Aunt Norah had been in any degree successful in these attempts, for Helena and the men concerned had eyed each other with embarrassed suspicion, both parties seemingly well aware of the situation. The thought of going through it all again filled Helena with distaste.

She free-wheeled down the long lane which led straight to the village green, where Aunt Norah's detached, stone-built house had a splendid view of the local goings-on. In addition to looking out on to the green, with its fine oak trees and weed-covered pond, it overlooked the inn on the corner which, though limited to local custom during the week, did a roaring trade on Sunday mornings with motorists from the surrounding district, especially since it had been used by a TV company as the setting for a film.

Helena braked and stopped outside the cottage. Rocky, her aunt's cherished King Charles Cavalier spaniel, danced around on the window sill barking a furious, ecstatic welcome. Helena had no need to announce her arrival by knocking, and when Aunt Norah opened the door Rocky rushed out and jumped up at her in an endeavour to reach her face with his long, eager tongue. She bent to stroke his silky black and white head before returning her aunt's kiss.

'How lovely to see you, Helena. It seems such a time! Put your bike around the side or when the kids come out of school they'll be taking a free ride, I have no doubt. All right, Rocky, calm down, there's a good boy! He's been restless for the last half-hour. I'm sure he knew you were coming,' she greeted her niece breathlessly.

Over lunch they chatted about family matters. Afterwards Helena read out extracts from letters she had received from her parents.

'You didn't feel you wanted to go with them?' Aunt Norah asked.

'Not really. I suppose it would have been interesting and I believe they have beautifully equipped hospitals, but I think I'm an English bird, I don't want to fly away. Anyway, I love Cornwall and coming down here to work is a great thrill.'

'When your mother said you weren't going with them I wondered whether you had a young man who was keeping you here.'

Helena laughed. 'You never give up, do you, Aunt Norah?'

'Well it's quite time you settled down. You're turned twenty-one and after that it's all downhill. Younger girls are coming along all the time,' the older lady said.

'Aunt Norah!' Helena exploded. 'We are living in the nineteen-eighties, not Victorian times. Marriage isn't the be-all and end-all that it used to be. Anyhow, what about you? You are always telling me what an interesting life you had on the district and bringing pretty nearly all Stipplewick into the world. Maybe I'll do the same thing,' she ended with a laugh.

Aunt Norah said thoughtfully, 'It's quite true, I have enjoyed my work. I've loved it all, going around the village, into people's houses, hearing their troubles—emotional as well as physical—and feeling that I've been able to help at times. And I've shared their good times, too. It's the most wonderful feeling, to deliver a baby! One minute it's just a swelling and a pain and the next it's a human being with a life ahead of it full of problems, happiness, the lot. It makes you feel a bit like God's servant. You've done nothing to make the baby but you have helped to bring it into the world. I loved that . . .' She rambled on.

Helena listened, fascinated. 'You've almost persuaded me that that is the life I should like.'

'Oh no! You see, it's all been very interesting but now that I am too old to do anything about it I realise that I've not got anyone of my own. Not one of those lovely babies was mine.' There was a wistful look in her eyes. 'It must be wonderful to be a wife and mother.' After a few moments she said, almost pleadingly, 'Haven't you got a young man yet?'

Helena smothered a groan. She had hoped to be able to spend all her free time here, she loved her aunt and Stipplewick, but if Aunt Norah was bent on continuing the search for a husband for her it was going to be impossible. If she confessed that there was nobody special in her life her aunt would start match-making in earnest. If she pretended there was someone, then sooner or later she would have to produce him. Helena felt in a hopeless position—until she had a sudden flash of inspiration.

'Well actually, Aunt Norah, there is someone who I am keen on—he's really great—but it's no good my even thinking about him because as far as he is concerned I don't exist. But can you understand that because of him I'm really not interested in meeting anyone else? Nobody else could match up to him in my eyes,' Helena tried to look as forlorn as possible.

Aunt Norah pursed her lips as she looked her niece up and down.

'Whoever this wonder man is, he needs his brain testing! Where could he find a girl with better looks and a nicer nature than you?'

'You don't think you could be the tiniest bit biased?' Helena laughed.

'Me? Biased? Certainly not. Who is this man, anyway?'

Helena thought with a sigh that she might have known that her aunt would persist in her questioning.

'Oh—a doctor at Trelawny,' she said with what she hoped was a note of finality.

Aunt Norah took no notice of that. 'Is he married, perhaps?'

'No, he isn't married, but all the nurses are mad about him. He is very attractive.'

To Helena's relief Aunt Norah then talked of other matters. But she brought the subject up again later on when they were walking around the garden. Gardening was a chore which had to be done but was not Aunt Norah's idea of fun. The garden was mostly grass and the beds had been planted with large flowering bushes to cut down on weeding.

She pulled up a root of groundsel. 'I remember when you were a little girl you used to pick every bit of groundsel you could find to take back to your canary.'

Helena laughed. 'Yes, I remember that. I used to think you had a beautiful garden because of all that groundsel! Of course, it was dead by the time I got home. Anyhow, I picked enough for an aviary.'

'You were a dear little girl with your big blue eyes and long fair hair. I envied your mother. I sometimes wondered why I tried so hard to pair her off with your father instead of trying to keep him for myself,' Aunt Norah said disconsolately.

Helena looked at her pleasantly rounded face and thick white hair and imagined that she could have been a very pretty girl. 'Yes, with your love of match-making, fancy leaving yourself out! I'm surprised you never married.'

'It was because I was very stupid. I had a young man, he was very good-looking, tall and fair-haired, like a Viking. He was the handsomest man I had ever seen and when he asked me to marry him—oh, I was over the moon!' She straightened up and stared into space with a straggle of dead flowers in her hand.

Helena felt a pang of sorrow. 'What happened, Aunt Norah?' she asked softly.

She looked at Helena with a defiant smile in her eyes. 'He was killed by a lion.'

Helena pulled a face. 'You're joking!'

'No, I'm not, it's the honest truth—although I can understand you not believing me, lions not being very thick on the ground hereabouts. And no, he wasn't a keeper or an unwary visitor to the zoo, either. He was a big game hunter, and that made him seem all the more glamorous!'

'A big game hunter? In London?'

She nodded. 'Yes, I met him when I was nursing at St Ann's. He came in with a fever he had contracted abroad and it kept recurring.'

'Why didn't I ever meet anyone like that! Do tell me more.'

'He was killed in Africa. We were going to be married when he next came home. The wedding was only weeks away when it happened. I was heartbroken as you can imagine,' Aunt Norah sighed.

'How dreadful for you. You poor darling. And you remained faithful to his memory for ever. That is a real life love-story,' Helena said dreamily.

Aunt Norah tossed the dead flowers on the compost heap. 'Nonsense! I made a martyr of myself for so long that I ruined any chances I might have had of a happy family life. It is true, we were very much in love—but he was killed. Looking back I realise how very foolish I was to let that stop me forming a good relationship with some other man. I had my chances but misguidedly believed there had only been one man for me. And what good did that do either him or me? If I had never met him I would probably have settled for someone else.'

Helena was silent for a few minutes, thinking over what her aunt had said.

'I can't understand why I've never heard any of this before. You would have thought Mother would have mentioned it, but she never did.'

'Remember, she was a good bit younger than me, only a child when this happened. And in any event, she didn't know. I never spoke to her about my feelings. She heard that Bruce was killed, but I don't suppose it made any impression on her. I've only told you because I don't want you to make the same mistake that I did.'

'Me? But I don't know what you mean.'

'Well, it's the same sort of thing, basically. You say you are in love with this doctor but he isn't interested in you. So just don't waste your time thinking about him. We will look around for some other nice man for you.'

Helena was appalled. She had only mentioned it to deter her aunt from her wretched match-making—and far from doing that, it had encouraged her. Having to meet the assortment of men she knew full well her aunt would round up from somewhere, would spoil her future visits. So it was with a lack of enthusiasm that she agreed that she would be coming to spend the weekend.

'Bye, Aunt Norah, and thanks a lot. I'll see you on Saturday then, unless my leave is cancelled— you know what hospitals are!' she said as she left.

Rocky, sensing her reluctance, whined and

pawed her as she climbed up on to the ancient
bicycle, as if begging her not to change her mind
and stay away.

CHAPTER FIVE

FRIDAY WAS a busy day in theatre. Helena liked the atmosphere on operating days, there was a feeling of anticipation and activity in the air. The patients who were not having surgery today or maybe not at all, watched the preparations with a macabre interest which made them lay aside their books and magazines and forget, for the time being, their own ailments.

Mr Tracy made his usual early morning round to question and check the condition of previous patients and to reassure those on whom he would be operating that day. He stopped at Mrs Coley's bedside. She was a thin, aging woman on whom he had operated for a double hernia. It had been expected that she would have been discharged before this, but her general health was poor and it had taken her longer than usual to recover from surgery.

'Hello, Mrs Coley.' He reached for her notes and studied the chart which hung on the wall behind her bed. 'Well, everything seems to be settling down very nicely. How do you feel? Have you any pain?'

'No, Doctor, not any more, thank you.'

'Good. Then I'll have a look at you. Nurse, draw the curtains please.' When he had finished his examination he replaced the bedcovers and smiled at her gently.

'So. How would you like to go home?' he enquired.

Her pale, tired eyes brightened. 'Oh, do you mean that?'

'I see no reason why you shouldn't if you go carefully and remember that you've had surgery.'

'When can I go, Doctor?' she asked immediately.

'Dear me, I feel quite hurt that you are so anxious to leave us!'

She raised a work-worn hand, then let it fall again. 'It isn't that, you've all been so kind, I've never known kindness like it before. But it isn't the same, is it, as being in your own home? It don't matter how shabby it is, not really.'

He patted her shoulder. 'Of course it's better to be home. So you have a word with your husband and you can go home tomorrow. All right?'

'Yes, thank you.' She watched him move away with eyes as devoted as a dog's to its master.

Helena followed in his wake with much the same expression on her own face. She felt good and warm inside from just listening to him and watching him. He had such a kind manner, such a charming way with him, and he treated every patient, whether she was old and wrinkled or young and attractive, in precisely the same caring, courteous way.

When Helena was giving out the milk drinks Mrs Coley said excitedly, 'Wasn't it lovely what he said! To think I'll be home tomorrow for the weekend. I don't like Sundays in here. The doctors don't come around, there aren't any operations and there's a different sort of visitor, not the usual ones. It's all a bit dull and strange. No, I don't like Sundays here.'

'Your husband will be glad to have you home, too.'

'Yes, I'll tell him today when he comes in and he'll tell my son to come and fetch me tomorrow. He's got a car,' she said proudly.

'They will be up all night getting the place ready for you, that's my guess,' Helena smiled.

'They don't have any need to do that, I don't care what sort of a mess it's in, I just want to go home.' She called across to the woman in the opposite bed. 'Mrs Conway, I'm going home tomorrow!'

Ancillary workers plugged in electric polishers for the floor and beds and lockers were wheeled out of the way of them and then moved back. Freshly made beds were prepared in readiness for the patients when they returned from theatre, blood samples were taken to the path lab for cross-matching and pre-meds were given, all in addition to the usual daily jobs.

Patients and nurses had to shout to make themselves heard over the hum of the cleaners and rumble of moving furniture, but eventually peace reigned. One by one patients were wheeled in from the recovery room and transferred to the made-up beds, which were warmed by electric blankets. Drips were set up where necessary and pulse rates checked. Automatically, patients spoke in whispers, although it was doubtful if noise would have disturbed the still drowsy patients.

The smell of lunch mingled with that of polish and lingering anaesthetics and antiseptics, and did nothing to make the ward's atmosphere more appetising. When it was cleared away Nurse Jelbart sprayed the ward with air freshener before the visitors arrived, bringing fresh nightdresses and tissues and talcum powder, and sitting silently beside their still sleeping relatives before tip-toeing back out of the ward.

'Nurse Jelbart, I'm off to lunch now. OK?' Helena asked.

She took the garden path to the dining-room rather than the covered way. It was good to get out in the sunshine, to breathe the fresh air and to hear the birds twittering.

Collins was ahead of her at the counter. She turned to Helena with a grimace.

'Toad in the hole is about the best thing on offer, but it isn't my favourite meal. What are you having?'

Helena glanced at the menu. 'The same, I think.'

They managed to get a table for two. 'So, how did your trip go yesterday on the bike? I bet you're feeling stiff!' Collins grinned.

'Not too bad, actually. It didn't take me as long as I thought it would. And of course it was such a lovely day I quite enjoyed it. All the same, I'll go by bus tomorrow because I don't have to be back until Monday.'

'How was your aunt? Pleased to see you I have no doubt.'

'Oh yes. So was Rocky, her dog.' Helena pushed her lunch around on her plate. 'I haven't got much appetite for this after what I had yesterday. She really is a smashing cook.'

'Some people have all the luck.' Collins looked rueful.

After a few minutes Helena said dolefully, 'Unfortunately she is up to her old tricks.'

'Who? The dog?'

'No. Aunt Norah.'

'This sounds intriguing. What are her special tricks? Handstands or sleight-of-hand?' Collins teased.

'Neither, I wish it was as simple as that. No, she is a determined matchmaker.'

Collins eyes brightened. 'And you think that's a problem? Lead me to her!'

'No, seriously, it's so humiliating. You haven't seen what she dredges up. And she is so pleased with herself about it she's like a second-rate conjurer who gets a rabbit out of his hat whether you want it or not. Honestly, it spoils everything, it sort of hangs over you. Every time there is a knock on the door I feel as if I'm a stray mongrel at the Battersea Dogs' Home and someone has come to look me over!'

'Cheer up, you never know your luck. She might come up with a winner,' Collins tried to comfort her.

'But I don't want to get a winner that way,' Helena protested.

'There can't be all that number of men left in Stipplewick by now. I think, my child, that you are exaggerating. Anyhow, I wish it was my problem.'

'I agree, she's probably exhausted everything eligible in Stipplewick, but she casts her nets wide, my aunt! She has actually promised—I mean threatened—to find me a "nice" man. Ugh!' Helena said glumly.

'It isn't a fair world, you don't need anyone to do that for you.'

'You try telling that to my aunt. "You are over twenty-one," she says, "and time is passing." I ask you! As if that isn't insulting. I've a jolly good mind to call the weekend off,' Helena threatened.

'And be like you were the other day, miserable because you had nowhere to go on your day off? You've got to think of future weekends.'

'Don't remind me,' Helena groaned.

'The trouble with you is that you are not thinking positively. Tell her that you are engaged to someone secretly and so put her off for good,' Collins advised.

'The brains of the girl!' Helena's eyes brightened. 'What a great idea.' Then she looked doubtful. 'The trouble is that she would want to know all the details—and you have to have a good memory to be a good liar. And she would insist on meeting him.'

'Well then, isn't there somebody you could produce?'

'You mean like Bill?' Helena laughed.

'No, *not* like Bill,' Collins said firmly.

Helena chewed her thumb. 'And where do you think I hide these stand-in-fiancés?'

'It is a bit difficult, I admit. I wonder if any of the nurses has got a brother or a cousin . . .' Collins racked her brains.

'Hang on, there *is* someone! He's an artist and he lives at St Ives. That's quite handy, too. I wonder if

I could persuade him to visit me at Aunt Norah's some time over the weekend?'

'Is he free? I mean, has he got a wife or anything?'

'I shouldn't think so. He's a down-at-heel artist and I'm sure he would more than welcome one of Aunt Norah's dinners. Actually, what you said reminded me, because his sister was a nurse at St Ann's and a bunch of us used to go around to art galleries and strange parties. I heard from someone or other that he had moved down to St Ives. I've got his phone number.' Suddenly Helena felt better.

'Well there's your answer. I always knew I'd be good for something.'

'And you are, my love. Thanks a million. Heavens, look at the time! Nurse Jelbart will be chafing at the bit.'

'Well don't forget to ring this chap,' Collins said as Helena rose from the table.

'Not likely, I'll do that tonight,' she promised.

When Helena got back to the ward the visitors had left, but their offerings of flowers and fruit lay on lockers and an occasional cup and plate had not been collected. She hurried from ward to kitchen and endeavoured to find vases for the fresh flowers. This was always a problem which could often only be solved by throwing away flowers that would have lasted a few more days. Another difficulty was finding room in small, overcrowded locker cupboards for gifts of toiletries and fresh nightdresses and bedjackets.

The television blared out at one end of the ward for the benefit of those patients who wanted to watch an episode of their favourite series and voices were raised to be heard over the sound. Patients dressed in a uniform of quilted nylon housecoats and fur-trimmed slippers stood around chatting to bed-ridden acquaintances as they awaited their turn to go to the bathroom.

Helena hurried to and fro with bowls of hot water in between answering the calls of patients. Beds had to be made comfortable by straightening plastic undersheets which had an uncomfortable habit of getting rucked up and pillows plumped and moved to a better position.

It was not until the ward was tidy and those patients who were able were seated at a table at the end of the ward waiting for supper, that Helena had time to notice that Mrs Coley, who should have been sitting there with them, was still lying down in bed. She went across to her.

'Are you all right, Mrs Coley? You had better not let Sister catch you in bed or she'll have another think about you going home—why, what is the matter, Mrs Coley?'

A tear rolled slowly down the woman's cheek and joined others which had soaked into her pillow.

'I won't be going home, they aren't coming for me,' she said with a choke.

'Why not? What has happened?' Helena bent over her.

'It's my Bert, he says he can't come tomorrow.'

'But what about your son? He's got a car, hasn't he?'

'He can't come either.'

Helena frowned. 'But—but surely—did they

understand that you were to be discharged?'

'Yes,' she sniffed, 'they know that. But Bert, he says he's going to play darts—'

'Play darts?' Helena asked in wonder.

'Yes, he's in the team, see,' Mrs Coley explained.

'And your son?'

'I don't know. But Bert says he—he wants to go to Plymouth for the day.'

Helena felt a hard core of unhappiness. 'Well, cheer up, Mrs Coley. Have a word with Sister and I have no doubt something can be arranged,' she said brightly.

Nurse Jelbart returned from her break as the buzzer announced the arrival of supper. She and Helena carried large containers of food from the lift to the kitchen, where Sister Bell was waiting to serve out the portions for the patients, naming them as she did so, for some were on special diets.

Helena and Nurse Jelbart took the plates into the ward where criticism of the meal was bandied to and fro, and Helena came to the conclusion that it would be impossible to please everybody. The pudding was ice cream, which was a favourite, but there was seldom enough to go round so some patients had to be satisfied with the alternative— which on this occasion was stewed plums and rice. The extent of ill-feeling which this aroused was unbelievable and only possible where the people concerned had little else to occupy their minds.

When the meal was over and everything cleared away it was the medicine round, then time to ensure that everybody was comfortable before the visitors came again. Helena was going off duty when she remembered Mrs Coley and went across to ask her if she had spoken to Sister.

'I asked her, Nurse, like you said. But she says she can't do nothing. The ambulance men are going slow and only dealing with emergencies.' Her voice was flat and lifeless and Helena was both sad and angry. She said a few useless words but nothing she said could be comforting. She hated to think of Mrs Coley still being there on Sunday.

She walked slowly out of the ward and along the corridor. Then suddenly she stopped and retraced her steps. She knocked determinedly on Sister's door.

'Enter,' Sister Bell replied.

Helena pushed open the door and wished that she could go out again, for Mr Tracy was also seated at the table on which stood two cups of coffee.

'I'm sorry, Sister, I didn't know . . .' she began.

'It's all right, Nurse, what do you want?'

Helena swallowed a lump in her throat. 'It's about Mrs Coley, Sister.' She glanced across at the surgeon. 'Mr Tracy said she could go home tomorrow and she was so looking forward to that, but there is no one who will call for her and—and she can't go by ambulance, apparently, because of the go-slow, so—'

Sister Bell looked at her coldly. 'I do know all this, Nurse Chamberlain. In case you may have forgotten, I am the sister in charge of the ward.'

'Yes, Sister, I know. But, well I'd like to order a taxi for her so that she—she won't have to spend

Sunday here. She hates that. Will that be all right?'

They both stared at her with unsmiling faces and she was embarrassed by the silence. At last Sister Bell said sharply, 'No, Nurse, it certainly will *not* be all right. What on earth do you think gives you the right to make such an arrangement? You are exceeding your duties.'

'I daresay I am, and I am sorry about that, but she was so looking forward to going home, and what har—'

'That is her and her husband's affair. Haven't you been taught that you must not become involved in your patients' lives?' Sister asked sternly.

'Oh yes, I have, and I realise that sometimes it can be wrong for that to happen. But in this case it seems a shame to let such a rule—'

'That will do, Nurse. You may go.' Sister Bell dismissed her coldly.

Helena gave a final look of despair at Mr Tracy, but he said nothing. So, after all, his pleasant caring manner was just a facade and he hadn't the happiness of his patients at heart. She felt bitter and disillusioned as she made her way along the corridor.

She unpinned her apron and chose to take the garden route to the hostel. She walked slowly, letting the cool breeze fan her hot cheeks. Helena had almost reached the doors when she heard her name called. She turned around and came face to face with Mr Tracy, whom she looked at with hostile eyes. 'Yes, sir?'

He leaned against the wall, a hand thrust into his

pocket. She hardened her heart against his un-doubted attraction.

'That was a very kind thought of yours, Nurse, but I don't think you considered the implications.'

'Sir?' She looked up into his half-hidden grey eyes questioningly.

'It would seem, you see, that this patient's hus-band and son both lacked sufficient enthusiasm at the prospect of her return home for them to make the effort to change their arrangements and fetch her. Indeed, the husband intends going out with his friends. So if Mrs Coley took a taxi home who would see to her baggage, make sure that the house was warm enough, prepare her a cup of tea or a meal? In the circumstances it would not be right to send her home. She is disappointed, and under-standably so, but this is a family matter and how-ever much we may sympathise with her, there is really nothing we can do,' he said quietly.

Helena's feelings of adoration came flooding back. 'Oh yes, sir, I do see that what you say is right. I hadn't thought of it like that,' she admitted.

He inclined his head. 'Doctors and nurses, pos-sibly more than most people, need to think very carefully before they act. Remember that, Nurse.'

'Oh yes, sir, I will.'

There was a humorous glint in his eyes, she felt certain. 'Good,' he said smoothly. 'Then who knows? One day we may make something of you.' He touched her shoulder briefly before he strode away.

She felt as if he had thrown cold water in her face. 'You beast!' she muttered through clenched teeth.

'I hate you, you sanctimonious, self-satisfied beast! I hate you. Hate you!'

She rushed up the stairs to her room, stared briefly at her scarlet cheeks, then relieved her feelings by thumping her pillow.

CHAPTER SIX

IT WAS quite late when Helena remembered that she had to make a telephone call to Bob Stevens, her artist friend at St Ives. It had seemed a good idea when she and Collins had discussed it, but now she was not so sure. Bob was a casual, easy-going young man who had been a patient in St Ann's, where his sister Ann was a nurse in the same year as herself.

After he had been discharged he had quite often come to hospital parties or get-togethers and became one of their small set. Later, Helena heard that he had moved down to Cornwall, partly because of his health. When it was known that she, too, was going down there, Ann had given her his phone number.

Helena was taking a great deal for granted in thinking that Bob might be willing to spend a day with her, and, more than that, to pretend that he was her boyfriend. She looked for his number in her diary, then shut the book again. No, of course she could not invite him over, the idea was ludicrous.

She went back to her room and started a letter to her parents. When she came to tell them news about Aunt Norah she paused and stared into space. Quite clearly she could see her smiling, self-confident face with a bevy of men grouped around her. With a sudden impatient exclamation Helena swept the letter aside, grabbed her handbag and ran downstairs to the telephone before she could change her mind.

By the time she had dialled Bob's number she hoped devoutly that there would be no reply and it seemed her wish was to be granted. But just as she was about to replace the receiver, not knowing whether to be pleased or sorry, she heard his rather breathless voice.

It took a moment or two for him to realise who was calling him. Then, as if to cover this lapse of memory, he was rather too gushing.

'Darling, how lovely to hear from you. Where are you speaking from?'

Helena told him and, after the usual preliminaries, said, 'I'm going to Stipplewick tomorrow to visit my aunt who lives there, and I wondered if you would care to meet me there for lunch?'

'Tomorrow?' he said doubtfully.

'I know it's short notice, but I'd be very pleased if you could make it.' She gritted her teeth in the momentary silence that followed.

Then he said, 'Thanks, that sounds great. Stipplewick, you say?'

'Yes that's right. About midday?'

'Yes, there is an hourly service from here going in that direction. I'll see you at the bus-stop, there's one in the square, I think, but I hardly think we'd miss one another in a place that size!'

'Good, that's great. Thanks a lot, I look forward to seeing you, Bob.' Helena replaced the receiver and made a gesture of relief tinged with finality.

She dialled her aunt's number. I really have got a nerve, she thought, as she waited for her to reply. Fancy inviting . . .

'Hello, Aunt Norah.'

Her aunt sounded disappointed. 'Now don't tell me you can't come!'

'Oh no, I can come and I'm looking forward to it. But Aunt Norah—I'd like to invite a friend of mine to lunch—I know it's awful cheek, but—'

'Nonsense, you know any friend of yours is welcome. Is it another nurse?' Aunt Norah was immediately curious.

'No. He is the brother of one of the nurses at St Ann's, who lives in St Ives.'

'Oh, you've made my day, I *do* look forward to meeting him. I was afraid your leave had been cancelled and I didn't know what I was going to do about my joint of beef, it's far too big just for me.'

'It sounds gorgeous. You are a dear. Oh, I haven't looked up the time of my buses. I hope I get there before Bob does or he'll think I'm not turning up. I think I'll try to borrow the bike again, unless it's raining . . .'

It was such a pleasant morning that Helena had a feeling of happy anticipation at the weekend ahead. She sought out Coe to ask if she might borrow her bike again. Coe said she seldom used it herself and would sell it to Helena for a fiver, so the deal was made, both girls thinking they had done well out of it.

Helena set off with a feeling of proud ownership. Once away from the town and the immediate outskirts, it was a pretty ride through lanes so narrow in places that branches met and interlaced overhead. As she passed farm buildings, loose straws of oats and barley torn from passing tractors which carried the harvest had caught and dangled from overhanging boughs. The air was heady and intoxicating with the smell of ripe blackberries mingled with the scent of hazel-nuts hardening in their shells.

On either side, the hedges, which earlier in the year had been a froth of pink campions and white wild parsley, were now more autumnal with St John's Wort, spikes of foxglove seed-pods and hawthorn bushes scarlet with berries. When the lanes led to an open tract of common Helena stopped in admiration. It was a carpet of purple and yellow, the heather and gorse in their second blooming because of the spell of good weather. She smiled happily. Surely nowhere in the world could be more beautiful or the air sweeter.

It was almost with a feeling of regret that she reached the outskirts of Stipplewick. It was a pretty village but in recent years the north side was marred by an estate of new, rather ugly houses and flats and some shops. Aunt Norah's house was in the unspoilt older part.

No sooner did Helena reach the village green than she heard Rocky's bark, and when she stopped outside the house he jumped from the window sill and rushed to the door in ecstatic anticipation. Aunt Norah was equally welcoming in a more subdued fashion. She kissed Helena fondly.

'Oh, you are a naughty girl, letting me go on

worrying about you, when you had a young man all the time! Why didn't you tell me?'

Helena gave a guilty laugh. 'Oh well! I do feel awful inviting him to lunch—'

'Why I'm delighted. I see you came on the bike.'

'It's *my* bike now, I bought it from Coe, she says she hardly ever uses it.'

'You'll find it very useful for coming over here, because the bus service is so bad,' Aunt Norah said cheerfully.

'That reminds me. Have you any idea what time the bus from St Ives arrives? Somewhere around midday?'

'I'll look it up in a minute. I'll just heat up the coffee.' She took the timetable from the kitchen drawer. 'Here it is—twelve-fifteen in Bridge Street. That will be the one, I expect. You know where Bridge Street is?'

'Yes, it's in the square, isn't it?' Helena checked.

'That's right. You've got plenty of time, it only takes ten minutes to walk there.'

Aunt Norah poured two steaming cups of coffee and Helena sniffed appreciatively. Everything here in Stipplewick smelt and tasted so much better than anywhere else.

'So you are engaged, then?'

Helena choked into her coffee. 'Heavens no! I—'

'I thought you wouldn't do a thing like that without bringing him to meet me first,' Aunt Norah went on, ignoring her niece.

Helena nibbled at a home-made gingerbread biscuit and hated herself for being deceitful. She should tell her aunt now, before Bob was involved.

She was debating how to word it when Aunt Norah said,

'It's a good thing you rang me when you did. I was going to invite a young man in to meet you.'

'Aunt Norah!' Helena wailed.

'Oh, I know. I understand now. If you've got a young man, that's it. But how was I to know? This young man is old Mrs Reynolds' nephew and he's just come down here to open one of the new shops, selling handbags and luggage.'

'Well, I'm sure he's had a very lucky escape. If you'd brought him here I daresay he would have taken the first train back to wherever he came from,' Helena reproved.

'Now why should he do a thing like that? I've not met him myself but Mrs Reynolds told me about him.'

'I expect he's going to bring down his wife and family,' Helena said.

Aunt Norah shook her head. 'No he isn't married, I made sure of that.'

That settled it. Come what may, Helena decided that as far as her aunt was concerned Bob was her young man—if she could persuade him to act the part.

She glanced at her watch. 'It's time I was leaving. Shall I take Rocky with me?'

He had known before she mentioned it that he was going for a walk. He raced up and down the hall, barking and jumping up at his lead, which hung from a hook in the kitchen.

'All right, Rocky, settle down, or we'll have to take you for lessons on how a well brought up dog should behave,' Helena said, fixing on his lead. He jumped up to lick her face and turned a somersault as he did so.

She set off along the green which was bordered by tall, detached houses separated by groups of tiny cottages. Rocky pulled hard on his lead as he strained to reach the trees and sniff the grass to discover which other dogs had passed that way recently. Helena arrived at Bridge Street early and wandered around, looking in the windows of the few shops, hurrying away from the butcher's as Rocky rushed up the steps to take a closer look and a good smell of the sides of beef that hung on hooks. She continued up the hill past the church, where she knew a different text was chosen each week to be displayed on the board in the forecourt. The pavement was narrow and she had to go to the edge of the path to read it.

The folly of fools is deceit. Helena was struck by its aptness and hoped it was not a warning to her. Rocky dragged at his lead, going as far as he could in every direction in his desire to sniff something interesting. There was a squeal of brakes as a car coming around the sharp corner had to make an emergency stop. Helena's heart thudded as she realised that Rocky was in the road.

She pulled him back on to the pavement. 'Heavens, Rocky, you'll get yourself killed,' she said and turned to apologise to the driver of the car.

'I'm so—' She didn't believe it. What on earth was Mr Tracy doing here? 'Oh it's you!' Her mouth dropped open.

His eyes were angry beneath his furrowed forehead. 'I know this isn't London but it only takes one car for there to be a tragedy,' he said.

'I didn't expect a car to come speeding round the corner while I was reading the text,' she said defensively.

He glanced swiftly at the notice-board. 'However, a car did come and you can consider yourself fortunate that I was *not* speeding.'

'Yes, I know,' she said, her heart having settled down. 'And I am very grateful to you for stopping so promptly. I'm sorry, I know it was my fault, but I'm not used to dogs and it didn't enter my head that he might run into the road.'

Miles Tracy also relaxed and smiled faintly. 'He's a very handsome little fellow, but you should train him. Cavaliers are very intelligent and learn quickly.'

'You'll have to tell my aunt that, he isn't mine. She thinks the world of him and if anything had happened to him I wouldn't have dared to go back.' Helena bent to stroke Rocky's long, glossy ears.

Mr Tracy looked down on her hair which, lit by the sun, seemed to have a dozen shades of brown in it. It was thick and shiny and small tendrils curled on her neck and around her ears. He could see the curve of her pink cheek and the slim outline of her body.

When she straightened up she was surprised at the intent look on his face and her blue eyes opened wide. 'Do you live here?' he asked.

'No, I have a flat in the nurses' home but I've got the weekend off so I've come here to visit my aunt,' she explained.

He was really smiling now, his eyes were friendly as they glinted between his thick lashes. 'Then perhaps you—'

A short blast on a car horn alerted them both. A bus coming down the hill was unable to continue in the narrow road until he moved on. He raised his hand in a gesture of farewell to her—or it could have meant anything—before driving on up the hill.

Helena watched him go. There was a cheated look on her face. If only that bus had not come at that moment. If only the road was not so narrow. What would he have said? Was he going to ask if she knew some place where he could have lunch? Or perhaps if she knew some person? At that moment he had seemed so friendly he could have been going to say almost anything.

Helena shook herself mentally. There she went again, dreaming dreams about a man whom she was well aware she must banish from her thoughts. With a start she realised that Bob would have been on that bus and she hurried back to Bridge Street.

It came as no great surprise to her that Mr Tracy was here in Stipplewick, for most of the hospital staff lived somewhere in the area. It came as no surprise, either, that once again he had caught her doing the wrong thing. It was strange that it always happened that way when she wished so much to appear cool and capable and self-confident as a good nurse should. Like Sister Bell always did. Helena wondered how friendly they were. In the course of their work they were bound to see a great deal of each other, but did their relationship go further than that? What *had* he been going to say?

Bob was standing at the bus-stop. Helena had not remembered that he was so thin—he looked all angles, as if his bones were forcing their way through his transparent skin. She hoped he had not suffered any further from the lung trouble that had landed him in St Ann's. Nevertheless, despite his emaciated appearance he looked stylish and good-looking in a lean and hungry way. She wondered whether he would remember her.

'Hello, Bob.'

His initial look of unawareness quickly changed to a welcoming smile. 'Darling, it's good to see you.' He touched her cheek with his.

'And you. How are you these days?' Helena asked.

'Just fine. St Ives is ideal for me, I spend most of the time out of doors painting, and love every minute. As my days are apparently numbered they will at least be spent in beautiful surroundings. Ten years there are worth more than thirty cooped up in an office,' he said as they walked.

'You do paint a gloomy picture of your own future. I'm sure it's quite unjustified! But I'm glad you are happy. How are you doing financially? Can you make a living out of your pictures?'

'I manage. I share a studio and any expenses, and I can have as much fish as I want from the boats when they come in. There is plenty of choice and it's as fresh as a daisy. Who could want for more?' Bob laughed.

'It certainly sounds ideal. I could do with a bit

of fresh fish sometimes instead of the inevitable cottage pie!'

'Cottage pie! I thought they'd used it up on me, don't tell me they've still got some left!'

'It's a different hospital, dear boy, and not so many people to feed. We've still got a few years' supply in hand,' Helena said brightly.

'Oh, of course, you're at Trelawny now. How do you like it?'

'It seems very nice, but there isn't a lot of difference between one hospital and another regarding the work. And it's good that my aunt lives nearby. By the way, I'm really grateful to you for coming to my rescue,' she added cautiously.

'Rescue? Did you say rescue?' Bob looked puzzled.

'Yes. I couldn't go into details on the phone, but it's to do with me, my aunt and a husband.'

A wary look came into his eyes. 'A husband? Don't look at me, dear.'

'No, you're quite safe! But just listen to this.' She told him her problem and ended by saying, 'All you have to do is to act as if you care—give me an occasional loving glance, touch my hand, that kind of thing. You can do that, can't you? It should be painless.'

'It all depends on what kind of thing,' he laughed. 'Of course, I'll never be able to keep a straight face, you know that.'

'Please, Bob, you must. It really is essential,' she said earnestly.

'Darling, it isn't really my scene!' he protested— and he sounded serious.

Helena stopped walking and glared up at him. 'Well then, that's your lot, I'm afraid. You had better take the next bus back. There'll be no dinner for you unless you agree to play your part.'

Rocky danced around and around his legs, determined to keep him there with his lead if necessary.

'Beat it!' he said. 'Keep that hound off my one and only decent pair of pants, for God's sake.'

Helena made no move to do so. 'So, are you going to do it or not?'

'What's for dinner?' he asked suspiciously.

'Roast beef, Yorkshire pudding, parsnips, sprouts, pota—'

'For that I will agree to do anything!'

She bent down to unwind Rocky's lead and as she straightened up he put his arms around her and kissed her.

'How's that?' he asked proudly.

At the same moment she saw a car driving slowly past. With a sinking heart she realised it was Mr Tracy who seemed to be searching for something—or someone. He stared from her to Bob, then, with a sudden spurt of acceleration, drove quickly on.

Helena stared after him with tormented eyes. Had he been hoping to see her so that he could finish his sentence? She gave an inner groan. He must have seen Bob kissing her and would undoubtedly get the wrong impression. Poor Bob, he had only been doing what she asked of him.

'That was fine, just keep it up. Only don't let's rehearse in the street,' she said. 'How is Ann? I must write to her some time.'

'She's in the pink. Did you know she was getting married?'

'No, how lovely! Is it to anyone I might know?'

'Maybe. Brian O'Neill in Orthodontics. Sandy-haired, wears glasses . . .'

'Oh yes, I do remember him, he was very pleasant and the kids loved him. When is the happy day to be?'

'That I cannot tell you, but they are getting married next month.'

'Ha ha, very funny. And that is no way for a man who is contemplating matrimony with me to speak, and don't you forget it! We're here now, as if you couldn't guess.'

Rocky was straining and panting in ecstasy at the prospect of seeing his beloved mistress.

Helena laid a hand on Bob's arm. 'You will do your best for me, won't you? Please!'

In fact he played his part well. A nit-picking producer might have considered that at times he over-acted, but no doubt he felt he had to give good value in return for Aunt Norah's excellent dinner.

As he did not know her Bob had no means of telling that Aunt Norah was treating him with less than her usual warmth, but Helena was very aware of the fact.

'How long have you known each other?' she asked dourly as they were eating their plum tart and cream.

'A year,' Helena said hastily. 'We met when Bob was a patient in St Ann's.'

'Has your work brought you down here?'

'My work? Some people don't look on it as work. I'm a painter.'

'Of houses or pictures?' Aunt Norah asked coldly.

'Pictures. Come to think of it, it might be fun to paint houses. I could do murals on the walls. You've given me quite an idea.'

'I shouldn't have thought you could make a living at painting pictures,' Aunt Norah said.

'I barely do,' he laughed.

Helena kicked him sharply under the table. 'You don't do too badly, darling. You are too modest.'

'I suppose not, I just about get by. I don't make enough to get married just yet, but one day, eh, darling?' His face was turned away from Aunt Norah and as he looked at Helena he crossed his eyes comically.

She choked over her pastry and he patted her on the back.

'There are jobs that are quite well paid in commercial art,' Aunt Norah pointed out gloomily as she brought in the coffee.

'Commercial art?' Bob frowned as if in pain. 'That isn't really me at all. I must be free to do my own thing, to paint what I see as I see it. I don't want to design a paper wrapper for a bar of chocolate or a packet of soap powder.'

'People who want to get married often have to do things they would prefer not to.' Aunt Norah's mouth tightened.

He glanced swiftly at Helena's warning face. 'I do agree with you. And although I prefer to paint what I like, I am, of course looking for work that will enable Helena and me to—'

She saw his eyes glinting dangerously, so interrupted him. 'And I'm quite sure you will get something soon, although it isn't easy these days. In the meantime, it's good that we will be able to see each other frequently.'

Aunt Norah fell silent, which was most unlike her. When Bob was leaving she made no mention of him visiting again.

He raised her hand to his lips. 'I'm so glad to have met you. And thank you for a marvellous lunch, Aunt Norah. May I call you that?'

She gave a terse nod and when he released her hand Helena saw her rub it against her skirt. Helena walked with him to the bus-stop.

'Well, how did I do?'

'You are a wretch, you tried to make me laugh and that would have given the game away. Still, thanks Bob, thanks a lot. You did jolly well. Maybe you should switch jobs and be an actor! I only hope it has put a stop to Aunt Norah's match-making.'

'I shouldn't think it was all that easy to stop her doing anything once she'd made up her mind. We could always have another try. Am I likely to get invited for another feed?' he asked hopefully.

Helena raised her eyebrows dubiously. 'Who knows? Let's hope so.'

But as she returned to the cottage she had to admit to herself that it was extremely unlikely.

'So that's your young man, is it?' Aunt Norah said grumpily as they sat by the fire later that evening.

'Yes. Dear Bob,' Helena said, crossing her fingers unobtrusively.

'Hm. He isn't the type I would have thought you'd choose.' Aunt Norah, not one to sit doing nothing, had some knitting in her hands but frequently put it down only to pick it up again, a sure sign that she was disturbed.

'We understand each other. And he is really very talented.'

'And he paints pictures for a living.'

'That's right. He has a studio overlooking the harbour at St Ives which he shares to help with expenses.'

'With a man?' Aunt Norah asked sharply.

'Of course.'

Aunt Norah stared morosely at the small fire which was more of a luxury than a necessity on this late summer evening.

'He'll never be in a position to support a wife and family,' she said after a while.

'That's rather a sweeping statement. Maybe he will paint a masterpiece. Anyway, artists do get married. Those at St Ives sell a lot of pictures during the summer to the visitors. They sell like hot cakes.'

Aunt Norah shook her head. 'I can't see him getting married.'

Helena laughed. 'That's only because you didn't choose him for me,' she teased. 'You just love being the matchmaker!'

Aunt Norah did not join in her laughter. 'I would have picked somebody more suitable, I can tell you that. It's my belief you are wasting your time on him. And he doesn't look very healthy either.'

'Well then, if nothing comes of it I'll always have my career. Maybe I'll decide to do district nursing. How would you like that? I could live here with you and we could discuss all my cases. Does that appeal to you?'

Her thoughts wandered to the morning when she had seen Mr Tracy. What *had* he been going to say? And when she saw him again—what was he looking for? If it was a place, he could have asked any passer-by. She, as a visitor, would be a most unlikely person to help him.

She cringed inwardly as she recalled the look of disdain on his face when Bob kissed her. She could understand his disgust. A hospital consultant would not care to see one of his staff behaving in such a way in a village street in broad daylight. She was not keen on the idea herself. But Bob was only acting a part to please her and would not have given what he did a second thought.

She might have known that Aunt Norah would not care for Bob, but in the circumstances that did not matter, it was difficult to know how she would have felt if her relationship was a sincere one. Suppose—just suppose that she had been able to present Mr Tracy as her intended!

Nobody could possibly object to him. But if they did it would not make a scrap of difference to her, for she would be the happiest, most contented girl in the world. As it was, to let her thoughts stray in that direction proved her to be the silliest. Especially as she had been warned by Nurse Lester. For what had she to commend her? She was a comparatively junior nurse, ordinary to look at, being fairly short and thin, with middling brown hair and the usual blue eyes.

In her favour she had her own good teeth, and whenever she saw the patients' dentures in dishes she vowed to do her utmost to keep them for ever, and a good complexion. But there was nothing in that little lot to attract a man who could take his pick of women; who was brilliant at his work; who had risen to the top of the tree; who had the most attractively rugged face and a magnetism which made every female heart beat faster.

There I go again, she thought with a sigh!

'Why the sigh?' Aunt Norah looked at her sharply.

'Just a sigh of contentment, Aunt Norah,' she smiled, and remembered again the text outside the church which warned all who cared to read, *The folly of fools is deceit.*

CHAPTER SEVEN

DURING THE following week Mrs Tonkin died.

'It wasn't altogether unexpected,' Sister Bell told Helena when she was presenting patients' case notes. 'She had a history of heart trouble.'

'Would it have made any difference if she had been operated on the first time she was admitted? She would have been spared a lot of tension and anxiety, wouldn't she?'

'Well now, Nurse Chamberlain, how do you expect me to answer such a question? I'll take Miss Salmon's notes next.'

Helena passed them to her, but her mind was still on Mrs Tonkin.

'But a hernia operation isn't . . .'

'The operation was straightforward and non-urgent. It was her heart that gave out. Mr Tracy did all that was possible and she was resuscitated a couple of times, but in the end—she could have died from a heart attack at any time, whether she had surgery or not.'

Helena frowned thoughtfully. 'It all seems such a waste. It must be very upsetting for the surgeon too, when he has done a good job.'

Sister Bell gave her a quick, keen glance. 'It is inevitable that we lose some and save some. We must give our thoughts and energy to help those who are still with us.'

Helena sighed. 'Yes, Sister, it's no good having useless regrets, I know. But it isn't easy, is it?'

'And whatever made you think that a nurse's life was easy?' Her eyebrows formed two thin arcs.

Helena laughed. 'I should know better by now.'

'You know it was a false alarm for Mrs Plumley?'

'You mean the lump was not malignant?'

'Yes. She is to be discharged today.' She gave a wry smile. 'Tell her to take her precious flowers home with her!'

Helena grinned. 'What? Take half-dead flowers home with me? They were fresh when I brought them in. I demand a replacement,' she said, imitating Mrs Plumley's autocratic manner.

There was a tap on the door and Mr Tracy peeped in.

He looked around the room in apparent surprise.

'No Mrs Plumley?' he smiled.

'I'm afraid we were being rather naughty, but Nurse Chamberlain was responsible for that piece of mimicry.'

Mr Tracy eyed Helena with amusement. 'We will know who to call on if we ever start a drama group, then.'

'Will you fetch a chair for Mr Tracy, please?'

Helena glanced shyly at the doctor as she went to get one from the ward. He took it from her and thanked her with a smile.

Sister Bell said primly, 'That will be all for the present, Nurse.' Helena returned to the ward and left them chatting together.

There had been a new admission during the night. A seventy-year old woman returning home from a church meeting had tripped and fallen against a grave-stone and knocked herself out. She had lain unconscious until the vicar, taking a short cut to the vicarage, had come across her. Her injuries had been dealt with by Dr Wood who was on duty at the time. He was by her bedside now.

'How are you feeling now, Miss Hobbs?' The concern in his voice was sincere and made him seem a different person from the brash young man who chatted up the nurses.

'Very shaken, Doctor.'

'That is only to be expected,' he said gently. 'But time will help, you'll see.' She nodded her head carefully, wincing as she did so. He grunted sympathetically. 'Have you got any pain anywhere?'

'It hurts me to breathe deeply, and that makes me feel exhausted.'

'I'll take a look. Nurse!'

Helena drew the curtains around the bed and turned back the bedclothes.

Dr Wood felt the area with practised hands. 'Does it hurt there?'

She gave a sharp gasp. 'Y—yes, that hurt. That's where it is.'

He covered her gently with the sheet. 'I think we'll get another picture of that.' He held his finger up in front of her. 'I want you to follow the movement of my finger, will you? Keep your head still.' He moved the finger.

'That's fine. How is the appetite?'

'I can't eat because my mouth is too sore, but I'm not hungry.'

'Well, that will be better in a day or two. In the

meantime I want you to drink as much as you can.'
He turned to Helena. 'Plenty of fluids, Nurse.'

'Yes, Doctor.' Helena opened the curtains.

'Goodbye, Miss Hobbs, I'll be in to see you again
tomorrow morning.'

As they crossed the ward he said, in an entirely
different voice, 'I'm having a party in my room
tonight, just a dozen or so. Why not come along?
On the second floor, number twenty-three.'

'Thanks, I'd like to do that,' Helena said, and
turned to see that Mr Tracy was waiting for her at a
bedside.

'When you are free, Nurse,' he said in loud,
censorious voice.

'I'm sorry, sir.' She hastily drew the curtains
around Mrs Penfold's bed.

'Hello, Mrs Penfold and how are you this morning? On the mend, eh?'

'Yes thank you, I'm feeling a lot better.'

He laid his hands gently around the area of her
wound. 'No pain?'

'No, not pain, but it's a bit sore.'

'That's only to be expected. Let me see, how long
is it now?' He looked through her notes. 'Well I
think the stitches can come out tomorrow. You will
find you feel more comfortable then. I expect they
are pulling a bit.'

'Thank you, Mr Tracy, it's lovely to think it's all
over. I'm ever so grateful to you, I'm sure. You've
been so kind, all of you.'

'You had a very trying time with the cancellation
and the further waiting.'

'And then having it put off even longer by eating

breakfast,' she said with a guilty smile of remembrance.

'Indeed, yes, that was very naughty of you and I've got a good mind to make you wait longer to have your stitches removed!' He gave her a reassuring wink to show that he was not serious.

Mrs Coley was standing beside her bed looking like a stranger in a thin tweed coat and shoes instead of slippers.

'So you are leaving us?' Mr Tracy said pleasantly.

'Yes, sir. My son has come with his car.'

'That's splendid. Take things easy for a while, no cleaning or lifting until I give you permission, you understand? You have got an appointment to see me in Outpatients, haven't you?'

'Yes, sir, in a fortnight's time. Sister gave me the card.'

A red-faced young man stood awkwardly inside the ward doors. Mrs Coley's eyes brightened.

'There he is. My son's come.'

Without going over to her he jerked his head towards the door and started to leave.

Mr Tracy picked up the suitcase which Mrs Coley was about to lift. 'Allow me,' he said, and took it over to her son.

'You have forgotten your mother's case, sir,' he said, courteously. The man turned around and glared at him belligerently before coming reluctantly to take it from him.

'Thank you, Doctor, you've been ever so good to me. And you too, Nurse.' She looked around at the patients in nearby beds. 'Goodbye everybody, I hope you'll soon be going home too.'

Helena watched as she followed her son out. 'That son of hers was going to let her carry her own case,' she said in disgust.

Mr Tracy smiled gently. 'You must not be too hard on him, Nurse. He was clearly embarrassed. Ah, there she blows.' He hurried away at the sound of his bleeper.

Helena went across to a patient who was sitting reading beside her bed.

'Mrs Elton, I see I have you down for a session with the physiotherapist.'

'That's right, Nurse, I'm waiting to go.'

Helena glanced at her watch. 'I'll get Nurse Jelbart to take you down when you are ready.'

For some reason, the day seemed endless. Later, when Helena went to the dining-room for her supper, she felt too exhausted to really care what she was eating and she hoped from the bottom of her heart that no one she knew would join her and enter into conversation. As soon as she had finished eating she went to her room and lay flat on the floor with her legs resting on the bed to ease her aching muscles. When she had decided to become a nurse it was working amongst and doing what she could to help sick people that had appealed to her. And she still enjoyed that aspect of it.

What she had not considered, and what no one had told her, were the hours that had to be spent on your feet and the back-breaking chores of turning mattresses and lifting bed-ridden patients. It was only to be expected that older nurses like Nurse Lester, who was away sick at the moment, and who had home commitments as well, were sometimes short-tempered.

Sister Bell was Helena's idea of an excellent sister. She was fair-minded, gave credit when it was merited and told the nurses off severely when they deserved to be. At times she could be very friendly. She was knowledgeable and all the doctors respected her opinion. Added to that she was young, slim and attractive. No wonder she was well ahead in the running for Mr Tracy's affection.

Helena closed her eyes. When she could summon the strength she would have a bath, go to bed early to rest her aching body, read for a while, then have a good long sleep.

There was a knock on her door. It opened and Collins put her head around it.

'Aren't you ready yet?'

Helena slid her feet from the bed. 'Don't tell me I've been asleep and it's morning already!'

'Clot! Bill is having a party and time's getting on. All his watered-down wine will have gone,' she said cheerfully.

Helena slapped her forehead. 'I'd clean forgotten! Oh, I feel too whacked—it's been such a day.'

'Rubbish! Never turn down the chance of going to a party, it may never come round again. Up you get. Shove your face in cold water and—' She came further into the room, opened the wardrobe door and looked around the rack of clothes. 'What are you going to wear?'

Helena yawned widely. 'I don't know. Pick something out for me.' She pushed herself to her feet and crossed over to the bathroom. When she returned, Collins was holding out a red and purple patterned dress.

'What about this?'

Helena pulled a face. 'No, I don't think so.'

'Well, I don't want to sound rude but you haven't got a lot of choice, chum.'

Helena looked with dismay at the hangers. 'Trousers, I think.'

'Have you got a decent top?'

Helena turned over a few sweaters and took out a blue cotton off-the-shoulder blouse.

'This will do.'

Collins whistled. 'I said decent! To my puritanical way of thinking that is definitely indecent.'

'It'll have to do,' Helena yawned. 'Maybe it'll give Billy-boy a thrill.'

The sound of music directed them to Bill's room. Several young nurses and doctors were already there and there was a great deal of talk and laughter. His room was one of the largest in the block and no one quite knew why he had been so lucky, but he took full advantage of the fact and frequently held small, informal parties. He had made the room very comfortable by fixing red-shaded wall lights, and in addition to a settee and arm chairs there were a number of large cushions scattered about the floor.

On the table there were plates of crisps and nuts and savoury biscuits. Cheap wine was poured into any convenient glass or mug and beer was drunk straight from the can.

Helena's head was throbbing. She took a glass of wine and some snacks on a plate and pushed a cushion on the floor between a settee and the wall. The hum of conversation, the soft music and the warmth sent her into a comfortable drowsiness and she felt she could happily stay where she was for ever. The snatches of conversation meant nothing to her but the atmosphere was pleasant and Bill an amiable host.

At last there was a general feeling that it was over.

'I'm on duty in casualty in ten minutes,' one of the young doctors said cheerfully.

'And I am on call,' said another.

'Night sister will murder me if I don't put in an appearance in the next few minutes, and I've got to get changed,' Coe said in a sudden frenzy.

One by one they left. Helena heard Collins bemoaning the fact that she had brought Helena with her and lost her somewhere. When they had all gone Helena pulled herself reluctantly to her feet.

Bill swung around on hearing the movement. 'Well, well, well, where have you been all my life?'

'On the cushion behind the settee,' she laughed. 'Was it very anti-social of me?'

He shook his head. 'Not if you were happy there.'

'I was. Thanks very much for asking me. I was nearly asleep when I got here but this rest has made me wide awake. Does that mean that I won't sleep tonight?'

'Hopefully, yes. I can think of better things to do.' He moved towards her with a lecherous smile.

'Oh no you don't,' she grinned. 'I tell you what I'll do, I'll wash up the dishes. How's that?'

'You're a girl in a million,' he said, and as she turned to collect some glasses, kissed her on the nape of her neck.

'Don't push your luck or I'll change my mind,' she said, hunching her shoulders and wriggling away.

She plumped up the cushions and moved the chairs back to their rightful positions. Then collected mugs and plates and carried them to the wash-basin.

'Is this where we wash up?'

'Certainly. Where else?'

She washed and he wiped and put them away in his cupboard.

'What shall I do with these?' She indicated the snacks that were left.

He found her a tin. 'Put them in here, they are my stand-by.'

She picked up crushed crisps and biscuit crumbs and threw them in his bin. Then she looked around with satisfaction.

'There you are, all traces gone. You could say it was as neat as a new pin.'

'Thanks, Helena, you're a pal. Did I tell you you were a girl in a thousand?'

'That's nice, that's very nice I must say. Before I did it I was a girl in a million. How I've been demoted!' She laughed and opened the door.

He took a step towards her and drew her into his arms. 'Of course I was right first time. You are a girl in a million,' he admitted and kissed her full on the mouth.

'Goodnight,' said a cold, clipped voice.

They both swung around to see Mr Tracy turning the corner towards the lifts. Helena's heart turned a somersault.

'That's torn it,' Bill said morosely. 'I've been warned about having girls in my room.'

'But this is altogether different. It was a party,' Helena protested.

'I know. But where are all the other guests? That's what Miles Tracy would ask himself. And why did one stay behind?'

'Oh gosh, I hope you won't get into trouble,' Helena said bleakly.

'Not only me, love, but probably you, too. Ah well, it's a dog's life, and I daresay we will both survive to be told off another day.'

'Bye, Bill.'

Helena walked slowly back to her room. It was really incredible. Why did she have to be the girl involved and to appear guilty when she had done nothing wrong? There must be a jinx on her, else why did she always appear to be doing the wrong thing when she came into contact with Mr Tracy?

CHAPTER EIGHT

HELENA'S next leave started on a particularly hot day. There had been no rain for so long that she did not fancy cycling through the long, dusty lanes. She decided to go by bus.

When she arrived, the door of her aunt's cottage was wide open and Rocky was sitting on the step panting in the sunshine, his tongue lolling, his eyes half-closed.

'Rocky!' she called.

Ashamed to admit being half asleep and so to have missed her approach, he continued to sit where he was, his only greeting the swish of his long tail.

'That isn't much of a welcome,' Helena said, fondling his ears.

He turned slowly and licked her with a lazy tongue.

'Oh you sleepyhead! Will you be too worn out to go for a walk later on?'

He turned his head aside indifferently, which was an answer in itself.

'Hello, come on in,' Aunt Norah called from the house.

Helena found her in the kitchen, standing at the table which was laden with savoury patties and vol-au-vents.

'Gracious, you have been busy. In all this heat,

too. It looks gorgeous. Are you having a garden party?' Helena eyed the delicacies appreciatively.

Her aunt gave a wry smile. 'What? In my garden? No, this is for a picnic.'

'And you've invited the whole village?' Helena grinned.

'Not quite. Sit down, dear, while I pack it up, it won't take a minute. Well, it's like this. Emily Greenhalgh who I've known ever since I was at school—we were best friends then—rang me up out of the blue. Pass me that greaseproof paper, will you? It seems she has come down here to live— well, in Panton, and that isn't far away. So as it's such good weather I thought it would be nice to go out somewhere for the day.'

'A good idea. But your Emily must have a terrific appetite!'

'I don't know about that. But her son will be coming too.'

Helena leaned both hands on the table. 'Aunt Norah!' she exclaimed in a warning voice.

'Because he's got a car.' She looked defensively at Helena. 'You can't go on a picnic at my age without a car, and I don't suppose Emily would welcome a several mile walk, either.'

'I do believe you are at it again! Well, this time you can really count me out,' Helena said determinedly.

'Hold on a minute, I'm not trying to do any match-making if that is what you're thinking. I don't know anything about her son, he could be married and have half-a-dozen children for all I know.'

'Oh go on! You must know something about him if you've been friendly with her all these years.'

'No, we only exchange Christmas cards. She rang me up for a chat as she's only recently come down here.'

'Oh . . . Well, I'm sorry. So long as you make it perfectly clear to Emily and her son right from the start that I am, as it were, already spoken for in the marriage market.'

Aunt Norah sniffed. 'Yes. Well you know what I think of *that* young man.'

'Poor Bob! You are mean, Aunt Norah, he is very nice and quite clever. Anyhow, I told you that the man I really am in love with is unavailable.'

'You mean that doctor?'

Helena nodded. 'That's right.'

There was an ironic smile in Helena's eyes as she said it. How terrible it would be if Mr Tracy ever had the faintest idea that she had woven such a fantasy around him.

'What time are they arriving?'

Aunt Norah glanced at the clock. 'Any time now, I should think. Well, this is all ready.' She packed the food in a large wicker hamper.

Helena went upstairs to the room which she now considered her own. In view of the fact that they were going on a picnic she was glad she had chosen to wear jeans and an open-necked, short-sleeved blouse. She washed her face to cool it and ran the comb through her short hair.

Although she had not spent a great deal of time out of doors, the sun had given her a sprinkling of freckles on the bridge of her nose and coloured her skin a pale gold. Hospital food, which was stolid and fattening, had not spoilt her figure, for the bending, stretching and walking, all part of her day's work, kept her slim. She stared at her reflection, not seeing it. She was thinking of the day ahead with a lack of enthusiasm. She would so much rather have had the day alone with her aunt, and taken Rocky for a walk. But her aunt was obviously looking forward to seeing her friend again and if that meant that *she* had to endure the company of some strange young man with whom she would probably have nothing in common, then she must do so cheerfully. After all, it would be no better for him.

Rocky was rudely wakened from his sleep by the arrival of a car and his frantic barking contained an element of anger at being disturbed. Competing with him were several voices and Helena went to the bedroom door and listened. It was impossible to hear what they were saying, but the voices were feminine. Of Mr Greenhalgh there was no sound. Heavens, was he going to be the strong, silent type who would be difficult to converse with?

She waited until she felt courtesy demanded that she put in an appearance, then she gave a sigh of resignation and went reluctantly downstairs. Mrs Greenhalgh was talking vivaciously in a pleasant, cultured voice. Her greying hair had been given a silver rinse which made it sparkle attractively. She was fairly plump but looked youthful in beige slacks and a floral top.

'Emily, this is my niece Helena,' Aunt Norah said proudly.

The pretty grey eyes lit up appreciatively as she took Helena's hand.

'How very nice to meet you.'

'Good-morning, Mrs Greenhalgh. I've been hearing from my aunt how much she has been looking forward to this meeting.'

'Do you hear that, Norah? Mrs Greenhalgh!'

Aunt Norah clicked her tongue. 'Oh I'm sorry, how silly of me. I referred to you as Emily Greenhalgh because that is how I've always known you. And of course, I never met your husband. It's Mrs Tracy, Helena.'

'You can see Jim in my son. He doesn't resemble me at all,' Emily was saying.

Tracy! Helena turned slowly. It couldn't be—could it? It was! She looked up at him and her face flamed. Emily's introduction was a blur of words.

Then she continued, 'Miles is at Trelawny hospital, that is why I moved down here. There seemed no point in him travelling to Harrogate to visit me when there was nothing in particular to keep me there now.'

He smiled down at Helena. 'We have already met.'

'Of course,' Aunt Norah said triumphantly. 'Helena works there too. So you must know each other well?'

'Not really. Mr Tracy is a consultant and I am a very junior nurse. As you know, Aunt Norah, never the twain shall meet.' Helena gave her a warning glance.

Her aunt, who on this occasion was not guilty of any manoeuvring, wanted to make her innocence quite plain to Helena. She said with a jolly laugh, 'Then Mr Tracy would know the doctor who Helena has quite fallen for. And I can tell you he must be really something for her to have done that.'

Helena would cheerfully have dropped dead at that moment. All three were looking at her as she stood completely still, every muscle tensed, scarcely breathing.

Then Mr Tracy said easily, 'I think that must be young Dr Wood. He is the nurses' pin-up, isn't that so, Nurse?'

Helena felt weak with relief. 'If you say so, sir,' she murmured.

Emily raised her pencilled eyebrows. '*Sir?* and *nurse*? We can't have that. It's Helena, isn't it dear? And Miles. You are both off duty now.'

Miles saw the colour rise in her cheeks and the way her teeth caught at her lower lip. There must be ten freckles on her tiny nose, and there would not be room for more. She had lowered her lashes and they rested on her cheeks like a baby doll's.

She suddenly glanced up and surprised a look of such intensity in his eyes that she felt her heart leap inside her.

'I took you at your word, Norah, and haven't brought any food. But Miles insisted on bringing some fruit and wine,' his mother said.

When they were ready to leave, Miles asked them if there was anywhere in particular they would care to go.

After some discussion they decided to leave it to him. It was plain that both Emily and Norah would be more interested in their reminiscing than in the scenery, no matter how beautiful. They were still talking as they climbed into the back of the car. Miles opened the front passenger door and Helena took her place beside him.

This was the most wonderful thing that had ever happened to her. It was a beautiful, sun-kissed morning and she was sitting beside Miles Tracy, a thing she would never have considered possible. With all the chattering and the 'Do you remembers' coming from the back there was no need to try and make conversation. Instead she could dream, pretend to herself that she was with the man she had fallen in love with because he also was in love with her.

She could imagine anything she wished. Perhaps he had just asked her to marry him and they were on their way to buy a ring. Or maybe they were on their honeymoon, the festivities over, and now going to a hotel. Soon she would be in his arms and they would be firm and strong around her and there would be love and tenderness, but passion too, in his eyes that were usually humorous or coldly angry. They would lie cheek to cheek and she would run her fingers through his hair. The imaginary bliss was almost too much and she had the frightening feeling that he might be able to read her thoughts.

She glanced at him as she pretended to look at the view through his window. He was again wearing his brown cord jacket, which further endeared him to her, for it seemed to show that he wore whichever clothes were handy without giving them a second thought. Yet she believed that nothing could have suited him better. He looked so casually comfortable . . .

She tried to imagine herself sitting in the crook of his arm, leaning against him. His eyes were slightly screwed-up against the bright sunlight and accentuated the myriad of tiny lines which radiated from their corners. She longed to touch them, to see if it were possible to smooth them away. Not that she wanted them gone, they were a part of him. His lashes were thick and curly, which was most unfair for a man who had so much going for him already, and they hid his eyes almost completely.

He had a V-shaped scar on his left cheek. Had he fallen from a bike or pony when he was a little boy and scared his mother to death? Or was it done on the rugby field? Or in a car accident? It would have needed several stitches. Could that have been what prompted in him the desire to become a surgeon?

As if aware of her scrutiny Miles turned to look at her and she glanced quickly away with a feeling of guilt. He was able to take stock of her. She was wearing a delicate, haunting perfume which he could not place. Her features were delicate too, with high cheek-bones, a tiny nose and sweetly vulnerable mouth.

It was that feature which he had noticed the first time they had met and on each subsequent occasion, and had felt an unreasoning, almost irresistible longing to kiss. When she had bumped into him as she went through the swing-doors to the dining-room her mouth had formed a soft pink circle of surprise and apology. When he had reprimanded her for some of her bad mistakes he had noticed, with a strange pull at his heart-strings, despite his very real anger, the way her lower lip trembled, and how she had tried to steady it with her even white teeth. It was seeing her in the square at Stipplewick, with a young man's arms around her and he bending to kiss her, that was the reason he was later pulled up for speeding.

He had told himself later that it could have been a relative greeting her affectionately. But on another occasion when he saw her coming out of Bill Wood's room late at night he had been consumed with anger. For Bill was no fond relation. There could not have been many young nurses who worked at Trelawny who had not been kissed by him—and probably bedded, he thought darkly.

His long, lean hands tightened on the steering-wheel. He knew that he was being absurd to imagine that a pretty, twenty-year-old girl should remain unkissed until her real love came along. But Bill Wood! Her aunt had said she was in love with him and that was understandable, for he was undoubtedly good-looking, highly sexed and experienced, with an easy, pleasant manner. He also had the makings of a clever doctor if he did not come to grief over some misdemeanour.

Miles Tracy shifted uncomfortably. He knew that he would have hauled Bill over the coals if it had been any other nurse he had seen leaving his room at night, and that was unfair. He hoped that Helena would realise that Bill was a philanderer. He didn't want her heart to be broken.

There was no pause in the chatter coming from

the back. At last Miles said, with a wry smile, 'Will they ever stop talking, do you think?'

Helena glanced at them over her shoulder. 'I doubt it. They have years of news to catch up on.'

'I understand they haven't met since they were at school. I shouldn't have thought there was all that much to talk about.'

Helena smiled. 'They're happy, that's the main thing.' They were driving down a lane which led to the sea. Miles pointed ahead to an old tower.

'That is Pengersick Castle. It was built in the reign of Henry VIIIth by a mysterious stranger who lived with a wife he hated. She hated him in return. They arranged a dinner to celebrate a reconciliation and each poisoned the other's wine.' He gave an amused chuckle. 'The wife took two minutes longer to die, so she had time to give her husband's body a hearty kick.'

Helena joined in his laughter. 'Now who on earth could have witnessed that?' she protested. 'Somebody must have made it up.'

He glanced at her sideways. 'No need for a witness. The post-mortem would reveal that the kick was administered after death.'

'Oh, of course,' she laughed, and wondered ruefully why she always appeared so ignorant when he was near. Sister Bell would never have made such an uninformed observation.

'Moreover, you don't query Cornish legends, you have to believe them if you want to know and love Cornwall.'

'Are you Cornish, then?'

'I'm half Cornish. My mother was born in Penzance and went to school there—with your aunt, of course, but my father was from Cambridge. I only came down here to work ten years ago.'

'You seem very fond of it. Do you want to stay here?' Helena asked.

'It's difficult to see into the future, but I should be quite happy to do so. I am very fascinated by the history and legends. I've made that my hobby.'

'You are interested in the past, not like Aunt Norah. She has always lived down here apart from a few years when she trained at St Ann's. She was the midwife in the Stipplewick area and she says that following the life and adventures of all the babies she brought into the world is far more interesting than reading about Cornwall hundreds of years ago.'

'I can understand that. Does midwifery appeal to you?' he questioned.

Helena thought of her aunt's advice to her that such a life was only second-best to having a husband and children of one's own. With Miles sitting here beside her she agreed wholeheartedly, but sometimes one had to settle for second-best.

'I believe I could enjoy it,' she said on a soft sigh.

He glanced at her dainty, shapely figure, her soft brown hair, and glimpsed her smoky blue eyes which now had a brooding look in them. He admired the invaluable work that midwives did, but he could not picture Helena in that role. He shook his head, unaware that he had done so.

'We are at Prussia Cove now, and this place is

absolutely choc-a-block with legends, chiefly about smugglers.'

'I can imagine. It looks very sinister with those awful black rocks. Just the place for smuggling, I'm sure.'

'Yes. There are lots of caves in those rocks, and that is where they stored their loot.'

'What an exciting life!'

'Until they got themselves shot. The customs officers were very ready with their guns in those days.'

'Who were the smugglers? Was that all they did for a living?'

'Certainly not, they were very often highly respected people who lived in the village. One in particular, John Carter, was known as the King of Prussia. He was a very religious man and a farmer. But he also had an inn on the edge of the cliffs. And you can imagine how useful that was.'

Helena sighed. 'Those picturesque days have gone.'

'Smuggling still goes on, of course. Whenever goods are heavily taxed or in short supply there are people who will try to get around that. You find it mostly at airports nowadays.'

'But that isn't nearly so exciting or colourful,' Helena said with regret.

'That depends. I don't suppose the customs men think of it in that way. Now we are coming into Marazion. If we can make contact with those behind us, I should like to enquire if they would like to stop here for lunch.'

'Easier said than done,' Helena laughed, as she

looked behind at them. 'Aunt Norah. Aunt Norah!'

'Did you say something, dear?' Her aunt leaned forward.

'Would this place suit you for lunch?' Miles asked.

'Yes, it's a lovely sandy beach and there's a wonderful view of the Mount. Would you like to stop here, Emily?'

'Yes, I would very much.'

'So it's unanimously agreed,' Miles said.

He drove through the tiny village with its winding streets. Palm trees grew unexpectedly in gardens near the beach.

'Shall we eat in the car or on the beach? We could probably have found a hotel for lunch, which might have been better,' he said.

'You won't say that when you have sampled my aunt's cooking,' Helena said loyally.

Because of the warm sunny day they decided to eat on the beach. There were still a number of visitors about and people thronged the causeway which led across to St Michael's Mount.

'Builders must have had a very hectic time building the cottages and the harbour and the castle, between tides. Just imagine getting all the materials needed across there, for a start,' Helena said sleepily when they had finished their lunch.

'No problem! When they were built the Mount was six miles inland. Since then it has been cut off from the mainland because of floods. There is a legend that the lost land of Lyonesse, which stretched from Penzance to the Isles of Scilly, was submerged by the sea. They say that the bells of the churches covered by the water can still be heard ringing at certain times. It is a fact that there were floods, and at very low tide tree-stumps can be seen between here and the Mount.'

Helena peeped at him from eyes half-closed against the sun. 'You know everything, don't you?'

He picked up a handful of sand and poured it over her bare arm.

'All right, I shan't tell you anything else. You shall go through life ignorant of all my facts.'

They lay back in the sunshine, comfortable and drowsy from the warmth and the wine. To Helena it seemed like a dream come true, and occasionally she opened her eyes a crack to make certain that it was in fact reality.

Miles rose to his feet. 'Righto. Siesta is now over and we will cross over to the Mount. It is open to the public today and we should be just in time for the tides.'

Helena squinted up at the high green pyramid and felt she would far sooner stay where she was, with him beside her. However, he stood before her, blotting out the sun, looking rugged and determined as if he might at any moment yank her to her feet.

'Mother—Aunt Norah—what about it? Are you coming to see over the Mount?'

They looked less than enthusiastically at each other and after a short consultation decided to stay where they were.

'But you two go. We will stay put. We're not as young as we were.'

'Indeed no. It's a strange fact of life that none of us is. However, I predict that you will both become grossly overweight if you don't do any exercise after eating that huge and delicious lunch. So don't say that I didn't warn you!'

His mother laughed. 'Then I'll settle for being big and beautiful.'

'All right. Be it on your own head. Helena and I will go by ourselves.'

Helena felt a spurt of rebellion. He had a nerve expecting her to do what he wanted without even consulting her. She had a good mind to refuse. However, his outstretched hand looked far too tempting, so she grasped it, loving the strong smoothness, knowing that it was his. She held it fractionally longer than was strictly necessary as they set off down the beach and on to the causeway which was still wet from the recently receded tide.

CHAPTER NINE

THEY JOINED the group of tourists who were gazing up at the formidable ascent ahead of them with rueful smiles. Seen at close quarters it looked far steeper than it had from a distance.

'Heavens, are we going to climb up to that?' Helena tilted her head back to see the castle at the top.

Miles glanced at her thoughtfully. 'Don't you feel you can?'

She looked around at the other tourists, who were mostly middle-aged.

'If they can do it then I surely can.'

They waited at the massive wrought-iron gates that separated the tenants' cottages and the harbour from the castle grounds. A guide dressed in livery unlocked the gates and greeted everyone cheerily as he took their entrance money. Almost immediately he began his talk on the history of the Mount.

'It is now the property of the National Trust, but over the years it has changed hands many times. The castle was a monastery before it became a royal castle . . .' His voice droned on.

'If you ever left Trelawny I should think you would be well able to get taken on here as a guide. I'm sure you would get your facts right and make it sound very interesting,' Helena laughed. Then wondered, with embarrassment whether she had been too familiar.

'You are too kind. I appreciate your testimonial. Tell me, in the far more likely event of *you* leaving the hospital, what work would you fancy doing?'

She remembered that Bill had said that his boss was eager to get rid of the nurse who had been responsible for allowing a patient to have breakfast before an operation. She remembered, too, the several warnings he had given her.

She said flippantly, 'I shall become a humble kitchen-maid at the castle and with luck and cunning marry the lord.'

He shook his head. 'You would be too late, he is already married.'

'Oh dear, then I could only hope to become his mistress,' she laughed.

He made no reply, and glancing up at him she saw that his face was set in serious lines. Hadn't he any sense of humour? Surely he knew that she had been joking.

The path became steeper and rougher and the guide worked hard at encouraging his flagging followers with well-worn jokes.

Helena stopped walking. 'You see that boulder?'

Miles nodded. 'What about it?'

'I am going to sit myself down on it and take a rest, and nobody will be able to do a thing about it.'

'A good idea. We can catch them up later.'

He sat down beside her and noticed with fascination the way the tiny hairs on her arms were like gold fluff in the sunlight. She looked extremely attractive and very desirable in her blue jeans and matching blouse, which was unbuttoned at the neck. He looked at her thick curly hair, the tip of her nose and the curve of her lightly tanned cheek and surprised himself by experiencing a fierce longing for her. It was more insistent than anything he had felt for any girl before.

She asked him some question but he didn't hear what it was, for he was too intent on watching her. Her eyes, a glimmer of blue, were smiling. Her throat was smooth and flawless. Her mouth . . . it was soft and pink and curved in a half-smile. He looked away and rose impatiently to his feet.

'Rest time is over. I think we had better try and catch up now.'

Helena felt hurt that he had ignored her question and now seemed eager to move on as if he were bored with her company. He seemed to have something on his mind. Was he wishing that Sister Bell was his more scintillating companion?

The path got even steeper and although she tried to keep up with Miles's longer stride her progress became slower. Her feet and back ached and she believed that the muscles in her legs would never be the same again. At last he turned and looked down at her with a strange expression in his eyes. Then he held out his hand to help her on the way and she took it gratefully.

'We must have missed a lot of valuable information from our guide,' she panted.

'He is probably telling of the giant's skeleton found in an oubliette beneath the kitchen over a hundred years ago.'

'Really? A real giant or just a very big man do you think?'

He replied automatically, but his thoughts returned to the night he had seen her coming out of Bill Wood's room and overheard Bill telling her that she was a girl in a million. He thought he knew Bill well enough to be sure that he would not be so enthusiastic about a girl who was there to discuss medical matters or hospital politics. He felt a great sadness, as if something very beautiful had been defiled. She could have been so exceptional, so enchanting. Damn Bill Wood!

'You do realise, don't you, that Bill Wood is a philanderer?' He spoke abruptly, uncharacteristically revealing his thoughts before giving them due consideration.

Helena was momentarily mystified. She couldn't care less about Bill's morals, so why tell her? Of course! Through Aunt Norah she had allowed him to get the impression that she was in love with Bill.

'I know he is fond of girls, he is quite open about that. But people change when they fall in love, don't you agree?'

'Maybe. But I think he has many years of flirtations ahead of him before he will be ready to settle down.'

'Who knows? Anyhow, he is very attractive and fun to be with.' Had she said too much or too little, she wondered? But she had to keep up the pretence of being in love with him.

He tripped over the roots of a tree. 'And you agree with people having casual affairs?' She felt the conversation was getting beyond her and was not sure what line to take.

'It's quite customary, whether I agree with it or not.' She turned aside with a shrug of her shoulders, hoping to change the subject.

He thought of the man who had kissed her in the square, of Bill, and of the casual way in which she had said she might become her employer's mistress. On that occasion she had been joking, of course. But was there an element of truth in what she said?

They continued walking in silence. He put his hand under her elbow to help her along and they paused at times to get their breath. A middle-aged couple had also fallen by the wayside and were leaning against a tree trunk.

'It's too much for us,' the woman said with a smile. 'Some of those people are a good bit older than we are but they seem to be managing all right. I feel quite ashamed.'

'Perhaps they are more used to exercise. It is quite a climb, but it's worthwhile when you reach the top. And of course it's downhill on the way back.'

'We've got so far we're not going to be beaten now. We are just getting our second wind,' the man said.

'That's what we've been doing,' Helena smiled.

They continued walking, all four of them, until they reached the forecourt of the castle where the guide was telling the party more of the history, how it had been the haunt of hermits in the fifth century. He spoke of Edward the Confessor, Henry de

Pomeroy, Lord Oxford and Sir John Arundel, and of the Cornish rebellion against the Reformed religion. Of how during the Civil War the Royalist, Sir Francis Basset, held it until it was captured by Colonel Hammond. That since 1660 it had belonged to the St Aubyn family but was now a part of the National Trust.

He led them into the Chevy Chase Hall where hunting scenes were depicted in the plaster frieze and showed them the splendid timber roof. In the tower, which was the oldest part of the castle, he pointed to a seat known as St Michael's Chair.

'According to the legend the husband or wife who manages to sit in it first becomes the boss for life. The same goes for an engaged couple. So who is going to be the first couple to make a run for it?' He looked around his party and his eyes fell on Miles and Helena. 'Come along now, sir, give your little lady a few yards start. Be a sport.'

The tourists laughed and urged them to do it, but Helena shook her head and turned away in embarrassment.

Miles took her arm as they began their descent. 'It's not only steep, it's quite slippery,' he warned her. Over the last half hour his manner towards her had subtly changed and some of the magic seemed to have gone from the afternoon.

'Are you afraid that I might slip and sprain a limb and have to go sick?' she asked harshly.

He beat his forehead dramatically. 'Heaven forbid! The hospital would undoubtedly fall apart without you.'

Things seemed to be going from bad to worse,

but she was glad of his support as her feet slithered and stumbled on the rough downward path. She was not alone in her difficulty, many of the party were grabbing at each other or at bushes while the guide tried to keep their minds off the difficulties by telling amusing anecdotes of famous people who had also undertaken the climb.

There was a concerted gasp as the man who had completed the ascent with Miles and Helena fell with a thud to the ground, his face a grey blur in a tangle of branches.

'Ken, Ken, what's the matter?' his wife cried anxiously.

He lay motionless and she dragged at the guide's arm. 'Please do something. Get help. He's unconscious.'

Miles strode over to him. 'Please keep back everybody,' he said authoritatively to the people who were crowding around him.

Kneeling on the ground he gently moved the man's head so that it was free of the bushes. He felt for a pulse, then immediately started cardiac massage and mouth to mouth resuscitation. Helena placed her arm comfortingly around the wife.

'He is a doctor. He will do everything possible.'

'He's not dead? Please God, don't let him be dead,' she murmured fearfully.

'He has had a heart attack. Has he had one before? Does he carry any pills with him?'

The woman shook her head. 'No—I—'

Miles glanced around. 'Helena, take over please.'

She continued with the resuscitation while he spoke to the guide.

'Ring this number. Ask for an ambulance to be sent as quickly as possible. Stress that it is urgent and that Mr Tracy has ordered it.'

He took over from Helena again and they worked together until two ambulance men arrived carrying a stretcher.

Miles told them what had happened. 'He is breathing again now, but I will accompany him to the hospital. His wife will want to come too.'

He felt in his pocket and took out a bunch of keys, removed one and handed it to Helena.

He looked at her questioningly. 'Can you drive?'

'Yes,' she said.

'Good. Then will you drive the car back to your aunt's house and tell my mother to wait there until I come for her. Will that be all right?'

'Of course. She can stay for as long as is necessary.'

'Thank you. Tell her that I will fetch her as soon as I am free.'

Helena nodded. 'Yes. Oh, but how will you get there? I will have the car.'

'No problem. I'll get a taxi,' he said.

He hurried away to catch up with the man's wife. Then he called over his shoulder,

'Thanks, Nurse.'

A hush had fallen over the tourists as they continued their descent. Even the guide deemed it wiser to keep quiet.

Helena heard them talking quietly to each other about the incident.

'What a lucky thing there was a doctor with us, I had no idea.'

'Yes, and a nurse too.'

'Are they husband and wife do you think?'

'I should think so. I noticed earlier on what a good-looking couple they made.'

'That poor man. Fancy having a heart attack when you're on a day's outing. A dreadful shock for his wife.'

'The doctor got him breathing again.'

'That doesn't mean he won't . . .'

'No. But he had treatment right away. He didn't have to wait for a doctor to get here. That made a lot of difference.'

'I reckon he wouldn't have stood a chance if he'd had to wait.'

Helena heard them talking but her thoughts and eyes were on the ambulance until she saw it drive away. Only then did she begin to think of the drive ahead of her. When she said she could drive she had not thought it was an appropriate moment to admit that since passing her driving test she had not driven at all.

Aunt Norah and Emily were still on the beach but were now sitting up as if they were ready to move on.

'Hello, Helena. Have you had a nice time? Was it worth the climb? What have you done with Miles?'

Helena explained what had happened and suggested that they went to a nearby café for a cup of tea before starting for home. She said she did not want one herself. Instead she sat in the car and studied the gears with horrified eyes. Fearfully, she turned on the engine and with a grating of gears drove slowly from the car park to the side of the road. She tried to remember what sort of a drive home it was. She remembered a small town with narrow streets and a fair amount of traffic. She swallowed hard.

She saw her aunt and Emily returning and attracted their attention.

'I didn't know you could drive,' Aunt Norah said.

Not wishing to make them feel as nervous as she herself did, she said with what she hoped was a confident smile, 'Oh, I'm a girl full of surprises! If you'll just direct me, Aunt Norah, I'm not all that sure of the way.'

Her heart thudded and her mouth was dry as they moved forward in a series of jumps.

'It's OK, just imagine we are kangaroos,' she smiled. 'It's just that I'm not used to this make of car. It'll be OK.'

She gripped the steering-wheel with damp hands and stared unblinkingly at the road ahead. To her surprise everything seemed to be going well and she relaxed, quite enjoying herself until they came to the town and she had to stop quickly to allow a juggernaut to pass. The engine stalled and she needed to make several attempts to start it before she was successful.

The journey seemed longer than she remembered and it was with a feeling of immense relief that she saw she had reached the green and Aunt Norah's house was just ahead of her. Rocky, with his canine perception, set up a frantic barking, and a smile of proud achievement appeared on Helena's face as she braked to stop. And then there was a horrible crunching sound of torn metal . . .

They all looked at each other in dismay. Nervously, Helena jumped out to see what she had hit. It was a stone bollard which she did not remember ever seeing before. She turned fearfully to the car and saw that the wing was badly buckled.

Emily and Aunt Norah got out to inspect the damage. Aunt Norah clicked her tongue and said what a shame it was, a lovely car like that.

Emily laid a hand on her arm. 'You mustn't worry about it, dear. Miles will be covered by his insurance. Thank you so much for driving us back. It was good of you.'

Helena gave her a grateful smile. It must surely be from her that Miles had inherited his charming manner to worried patients.

As she helped her aunt to prepare a light supper she joined in the conversation when necessary, but she could still seem to hear the sound of the crash and see the damaged wing. She dreaded having to tell Miles what she had done. He would think, and quite rightly, that she was completely useless.

CHAPTER TEN

WHEN MILES phoned later that night it was to say he would not be returning until the next morning.

'So I'll make up a bed for you, Emily. It's an unexpected treat that you can stay,' Aunt Norah said when she had put down the receiver.

'That is most awfully kind of you, Norah, but I do feel that we are imposing on you. Perhaps I could ring for a taxi to take me home?'

'You'll do nothing of the kind, my dear. I'm only too delighted to have you here. I'm just sorry that the reason is a sad one. I wonder how the man is doing?'

'I should think he is holding his own. If he had died there would be no need for Miles to stay,' Helena pointed out.

'How lucky for him that Miles happened to be there and was able to treat him immediately. It was good of him to go in the ambulance—that was surely beyond the call of duty,' Aunt Norah said.

Mrs Tracy's pretty grey eyes shone with maternal pride. 'Miles is like that. He will always put what he believes to be right first. Of course the ambulance men could have coped until they got him to hospital but Miles wouldn't look at it that way.'

Helena thought of the staff who were on duty. 'Dr Jones is a very good doctor but lacks Miles's experience. Him being there could make the difference between losing or saving the patient if it was an extreme case.'

Aunt Norah nodded. 'You must be very proud of him, Emily.'

She looked wistful. 'He is so like his father was.'

'Was your husband a doctor too?' Helena asked.

'Yes, dear, he was a GP. And very popular in Harrogate where he practised. The patients thought the world of him. You wouldn't believe the number of wreaths and sprays at his funeral. They lined the pavement leading to the church. And that was packed. Some people had to go into a side room and hear the service relayed there.'

'Knowing that he was so well-liked must have been a great comfort to you,' Norah said.

'Yes indeed. And so was Miles. Do you know, he wrote a personal letter to every person who sent flowers and there must have been well over a hundred. How he found the time I don't know, because he saw to all my affairs too, on top of his own demanding work. But that's Miles. If necessary I think he would go without food or sleep to do what he considered he must do.'

Norah gave a small sigh. 'What a lovely son to have! You are very fortunate, Emily. He will make some lucky girl a wonderful husband.'

Helena looked at her aunt in alarm and said hastily, 'A better surgeon than husband, I should imagine. A wife would have to take second place and not all girls would be prepared to do that.'

Emily nodded agreement. 'You are quite right, Helena, it could be a difficult relationship, unless his wife was also a doctor or someone equally dedicated to medicine.'

Like a sister, Helena thought bleakly.

'Is he thinking of getting married? Has he got a special girl in mind?' Norah, as usual, felt it was her right to know.

Emily gave her a cool, appraising look which reminded Helena vividly of her son. 'I have no idea, Norah, he does not confide in me details of his private life.' She smiled gently to soften her words.

Later, when she was in bed, Helena was wide awake in the moonlit room and her mind went over the happenings of the day. It seemed almost a lifetime since she had left Trelawny, a mere twelve hours ago. She had not known then of the thrill in store for her, that she would spend a day in Miles' company as if he were a friend. She could still feel his firm, strong hand on hers as he helped her climb the steep hill, and her proud embarrassment when they had been mistaken for a couple by the guide and some of the tourists.

She sighed. If only that were true! She basked in that dream for a while until she remembered his changed manner when they spoke of Bill Wood. She knew that Miles had been thinking only of her well-being when he had warned her about Bill and his many girlfriends. But she could hardly admit that he meant nothing to her when this morning she had allowed them all to believe that Bill was the doctor with whom she was in love. So she had said what she thought was best and confessed that although she knew he was flirtatious she nevertheless found him attractive.

Now, thinking back, and with hindsight, she wondered whether she had given Miles the wrong impression of herself. She caught her breath. Especially as he had also seen her being kissed by Bob. She turned restlessly and thumped her head on the pillow. That text was all too true—*The folly of fools is deceit.*

If only she had not crashed his car. If she had stopped a second earlier it would not have happened. She pulled the sheet over her face to shield it from the bright moonlight. All she wanted to do was sleep and forget that tomorrow she must face him and suffer his anger and disgust. His opinion of her could only sink to a new low . . .

Miles leaned back in the taxi, glad to relax after spending most of the night in theatre. By passing a sheathed wire into the man's vein, and so to the affected ventricle, the electrical current which passed through it had stimulated his pulse back to normal. Miles felt fairly confident that soon he would be able to fit him with a pacemaker and send him home. He felt a warm glow of well-being at a job satisfactorily concluded.

He glanced out of the window at the hedges laden with heavy clumps of ripe blackberries. When the rain came they would be ruined, but there was no sign of a break in the weather yet. He could not remember there being such a warm September before.

Despite certain doubts he had a feeling of happy anticipation at the prospect of seeing Helena again. He pictured her slim, shapely body which was the most seductive he had come across in many years of dealing with women. Her every movement fascinated him. Her hair made his fingers itch to touch it. The colour was elusive, neither golden nor auburn nor dark brown, but a mixture of all three depending on the strength of the sunlight. Her high cheekbones, tiny nose and tilted chin bewitched him. She was so lovely, so delicate, that he felt a burning anger that she had allowed herself to be used indiscriminately by men like Bill Wood.

He raised his eyebrows in faint humour. He was beginning to sound like a jealous fiancé. He gave a short laugh. Heavens, no! He had no intention of getting married to a rather hopeless young nurse who had many lovers.

But he longed for her. He chewed his thumb as he pictured her thoughtful eyes and the sweetly vulnerable mouth which belied her character. He stretched his long legs. If Bill and the man in the square, to mention just two men, could enjoy her favours, then why not he? Indeed he must do so, for only then could he hope to get her out of his system . . .

Rocky slid along the hall, barking furiously. 'I expect that's Miles now,' Aunt Norah said and opened the door to look out.

He paid off the taxi and smiled a greeting to her.

'Come along in, angel of mercy,' Aunt Norah said. 'How is the patient?'

'He's doing well, we're very pleased with him.' He laid his hand on Norah's arm. 'I hope you will forgive me for asking if Mother could stay overnight.'

'Forgive you? I was only too delighted. Even now we haven't caught up on all our news. You forget, it's been a long time.'

Helena, on hearing Miles's voice, had felt suddenly overcome with weakness and had hurried into the kitchen. She wanted to stay there, to put off the dread moment of telling him what had happened to his car. She decided to make some coffee and turned the gas low, but she could not stay there for ever. She went to the kitchen door and listened until they were deep in conversation before plucking up courage to take the coffee in to them. Her heart did its usual lurch and her eyes blurred on seeing Miles.

She went behind him and placed a cup on the table beside him. She was moving swiftly away, hoping that she had been unnoticed, but he reached out and, laying a detaining hand on her, finished what he was saying, then turned to her with an inscrutable smile.

'Thank you for your help yesterday and for driving my car back here. It was very good of you.'

If only she could have deserved his praise! 'Oh I—I'm afraid . . .'

Norah was taking Emily into the next room to show her some old photographs. At the door Emily turned back.

'We had a slight accident, Miles. You must not be angry.'

He looked at Helena. 'An accident? What happened?'

Helena ran the tip of her tongue across her lips.

'I'm sorry. I—I didn't remember it was there,' she stammered.

He drew his dark brows together. 'What was it you didn't remember?'

'The stone—stone bollard thing. It's outside, on the verge.'

He went over to the window. After a moment he said, 'So you drive from memory, not by what you see. So if a child or old person happened to be standing there but had not been there previously, you would consider it quite in order to run them down?' He looked at her with expressionless eyes, noticing the rise and fall of her breasts and the tremor of her lips. He despised himself for his quickening desire for her.

'Of course not,' she said with a spurt of anger. Then, realising the fairness of what he said, her anger fled. 'I'm sorry, I should have seen it, of course.'

He looked again at his car, at the dented wing. 'How long have you been driving?'

'D—driving?'

He stared at her in amazement, but made no reply.

A shudder rippled through her. 'Oh—you mean how long have I been able to drive?' He silently inclined his head.

'Well, no time really.'

He noticed the glimmer of her blue eyes before she looked away from him again.

'What are you saying? Surely you are qualified to drive?' He sounded horrified.

'Oh yes, of course I am. I drove here.'

'I see you did,' he said drily. 'As a matter of interest, when did you pass your test?'

'S—six months ago.'

'That's quite a time,' he said.

'I—I haven't driven since,' she admitted.

His eyes blazed. 'Then why on earth didn't you say so yesterday?'

She looked down at the floor. 'Well, when you've passed your test you should be able to drive anything, I thought. And—and I knew that you wanted to go in the ambulance with the man.'

There was a silence and she glanced up at him nervously. To her surprise he did not look angry. Instead there was a warm, almost compassionate expression in his eyes. But his voice, when he spoke, belied the expression.

'So you took a risk with three people's lives?'

'No—not really. I knew I'd have to drive carefully. I didn't think there would be any problem.'

'Exactly. You never do think, do you?' he said sternly.

Miserably she knew that once again she had shown herself to be incompetent. Never before she met him had she seemed so inept. At St Ann's she had been considered a good and capable nurse.

'I'm sorry, I really am. I wouldn't have damaged your lovely car for anything. I drove so carefully all the way here, and I honestly never noticed that bollard before.'

He turned from the window and surprised them both by putting an arm around her shoulders.

'Don't worry about the car, I'm just thankful that

nobody was hurt. It was very plucky of you to drive a large, strange car here in the circumstances.'

Her body sprang alive at his touch. Without any intention of doing so, she turned towards him within the circle of his arms and looked up at him with relief and gratitude in her lovely blue eyes.

He fought back a rising desire to kiss them and then her pretty mouth. He moved away.

'Plucky, but misguided—as usual,' he said coolly.

She felt as if he had suddenly slapped her face. It seemed he was incapable of being amiable to her for more than a few minutes at a time. No sooner did he say something pleasant than he had to countermand it by being scathing.

So maybe she wasn't clever like he and Sister Bell were, but that did not make her a complete idiot. The only idiotic thing about her was that at times she was afraid she might be falling in love with him, despite Nurse Lester's warning. But that was something she could grow out of, and very quickly at that, if she had much more to do with him.

He took a sip of coffee and pulled a face of distaste.

'Is something wrong with it?' she asked.

'It isn't very hot, but it's up to hospital standard.'

Knowing the general opinion of the hospital brew she felt suddenly furious with him and with herself. Snatching up the cup she took it into the kitchen and re-heated it, then took it back and slammed it on the table.

'I hope it scalds you,' she muttered under her breath, unaware that he could hear.

'I shall take care that it doesn't,' he said amiably. 'And thank you for re-heating it, that was good of you.'

Norah and Emily came back into the room and it was decided that when Miles drove his mother home he would return to the hospital from there.

'How are you getting back? Did you come by bike?' he asked Helena.

'No, she came by bus. Two buses actually, it's a long trip,' Norah said before Helena could reply.

'Then come back with us,' he said.

Helena flushed. 'No thank you. I quite enjoy the bus ride.'

'Please come with us, it will be nice to have your company,' Mrs Tracy said gently.

Helena smiled at her. 'That is very kind of you, if you are sure you don't mind.'

It was a round trip from Stipplewick to Trelawny via Panton, through wild and desolate countryside. Helena was surprised that Mrs Tracy could countenance living here after Harrogate. She herself would have found it unbearably lonely. They passed nobody and no traffic on the journey.

'Do you like solitude?' Helena asked in amazement.

'It is rather off the map, but wait until you see my house.'

They came to a group of about a dozen newly-built houses set in what appeared to be a private estate. They drove slowly between massive rhododendron bushes and trees. A pheasant picked his way daintily across the grass and his mate crossed the road in front of them in something of a hurry. They passed a small church, a dairy and a group of cottages before stopping before one of the new houses which looked out over fields to stables.

'What a charming place,' Helena exclaimed.

'I think so. This estate belongs to Lord Lethby. The cottages and dairy and church were built years ago for the workers. Recently, after paying exorbitant death duties, the new lord had these private houses built to help with his finances. When Miles saw them he guessed, quite rightly, that I would like to live in one of them. It is very pleasant here, there is quite a communal life and the church is full on Sundays.'

'How lovely! I don't imagine you could find anywhere nicer.'

'See what you think of the inside.'

It was attractively furnished with some nice pieces of antique furniture and china. There were also comfortable, more modern chairs and settees, and everywhere there were bowls of tastefully arranged flowers.

After they had had drinks and made a tour of the house, Miles and Helena left. Mrs Tracy kissed her goodbye.

'I hope we will be seeing a great deal more of you, my dear. Perhaps you and your aunt could come here for a weekend some time, we must try and arrange it.'

'Yes, it was a pleasant weekend. I like your aunt very much,' Miles said, as they drove away.

'She is very special to me. My parents are in Kuwait and Aunt Norah is my only relative in this country. I love her very much.'

They drove along the open moors. They looked magical in the light of the moon, which made the trees appear black and silver and still. Helena basked in the beauty of the surroundings and in the knowledge that Miles was sitting beside her. She felt she would have liked the journey to last for ever. But inevitably they were nearing the end of the trip. When they reached a small town which boasted a double row of shops, now closed for the night, Miles drew up outside a corner building which had a brass plate on the wall with the name of a dental surgeon on it.

Helena looked at him questioningly. 'Is this your day-time job?'

'No. Neither have I got a raging toothache. The dentist is a friend of mine who lives outside the village—his wife objected to living over the shop, wise girl—so I rent the flat above the surgery from him. Come up and have a look.'

He came around the car and opened the door. They entered at the side of the building and went up a flight of stairs to the large, comfortable living-room, which looked out on to the street. The walls were book-lined and there was a large writing desk and table as well as a comfortable settee and armchairs.

'It looks nice and lived-in,' Helena said. 'You didn't consider bringing your mother to live with you here?'

He shook his head. 'No, it isn't big enough for both of us and Mother wanted to keep some of her furniture and favourite bits and pieces from home.

Now what would you like to drink? Coffee or something stronger?'

He bent down to switch on the electric fire.

'Coffee would be nice. Would you like me to make it?'

There was an ironic gleam in his eyes. 'Thank you, but no. I tried your coffee this morning.'

'Oh!' She sat down on the settee, quite pleased to be waited on and not offended by his remark, for she guessed that he was teasing. 'You don't think I can do anything right, do you?'

He stood in the doorway which led to the kitchen, one hand in his pocket. He looked so attractive that her heart lurched.

'On the contrary, I feel confident that you are very accomplished at some things,' he murmured.

She felt unbelievably flattered by his remark. 'But you can't quite think what those things are,' she laughed.

'I hope time will put that right.' He disappeared into the kitchen.

She leaned back against the cushions and stared blissfully at the mock flames that flickered around the logs in the fireplace. This was happiness that she had never dreamed of, to be here alone with Miles in his flat and on such friendly terms.

'Black or white?' he called from the kitchen.

'White please. No sugar.' She moved a medical journal from a side table to make room for her cup.

'Are you hungry?'

'No, thank you. After I've been at Aunt Norah's I don't need to eat for a week.'

'I know what you mean, she's a jolly good cook.

Do you like music with your coffee?'

'I'm not fussy,' she smiled.

He sorted through a collection of cassettes, then chose some romantic piano music. 'Is that OK for you?'

'Mm, yes, lovely and dreamy. I wish I could play like that.'

He sat beside her, his arm resting on the back of the settee. The music was haunting and the wall lights were dim. Happiness, comfort and warmth made Helena drowsy and her eyelids drooped. She was almost asleep when she felt something gently touch her cheek. She remained motionless, pretending to be asleep, glorying in the delight of his closeness. His arm was now around her shoulders and his firm cheek was pressed against hers. Without intending to do so, she stirred in his arms and instinctively turned her face to his. Opening her eyes she gazed at him adoringly.

'Like the sleeping princess, you were awakened by a kiss,' he said in a gentle, teasing voice, and kissed her on the tip of the nose.

She laughed and rubbed it with her hand. 'That tickled,' she said.

He placed tiny kisses on her forehead and cheeks and she wriggled her head away, laughing.

'I'll teach you to laugh at me!'

He held her face between his strong, smooth hands and brought his mouth down on hers cruelly hard. His body, which so often she had longed to touch, was taut and strong against her and she felt a tide of urgent desire flood over her. He moved his hands over her caressingly, expertly, sending shudders of exquisite joy through every part of her.

More than anything she had ever experienced or even imagined, she wanted him, she was drowning in a sea of desire for him and her senses were reeling. At last, exhausted, they released one another. She gave a long sigh, a mixture of contentment and longing.

His eyes were smoky grey with passion. No wonder she had so many boyfriends!

'I was quite right when I said you were no doubt accomplished at some things. You are. And I've discovered what they are.' He smiled and kissed her again.

The pleasure which had been flowing through Helena's veins like wine, suddenly stopped at his tone of voice. She didn't know exactly what it was, but there was a hardness in it and this kiss was passionate without the previous tenderness. Was he implying that kissing and love-making were her only accomplishments? But accomplishment meant experience. Was he thinking of Bill? Of Bob? Her eyes stung as disillusionment and shame gripped her. She pulled away from him.

'It is time I was getting back. It's very late and I'm on duty early in the morning,' she said miserably.

He drew her to him again. His hands were like fire on her back as he pressed her close. Her heart beat so furiously it almost prevented her breathing as he took possession of her mouth.

After a while he said softly, 'I'll see that you are back in time and nobody will be any the wiser. I'll order a taxi for you at six a.m.'

The blood which had coursed through her body

like a flame now receded and left her cold and shaking. She felt humiliated to her very core. The 'nobody will be any the wiser' was the ultimate insult. The pride and happiness she had felt by just being with him had been enough, for she had never expected more. Now that was gone and she felt as if she had been brutally assaulted.

She rose from the settee on trembling legs and, drawing herself to her full height of five foot four inches, said, 'I want to get back tonight. Will you please order me a taxi?' Her voice was clipped and cold.

So she was playing hard to get, Miles decided. Up to a point that could be fun but, taken too far, it was tedious. With his hands gripping her shoulders, he forced her head back and kissed her roughly on her mouth.

'Don't tease me, Helena. You know quite well that you would thoroughly enjoy going to bed with me—and I freely admit that I would also enjoy it. So why this pretended reluctance? What must I do to persuade you? Do you like a fight?'

He had no feelings of love for her, that was plain. He had never mentioned the word. He had seen her coming from Bill's room late at night, seen her being kissed by Bob in broad daylight, and assumed the worst. Undoubtedly he thought she was fair game, an easy lay, especially as she had returned his kisses so passionately. Helena was bitterly ashamed of her uncontrolled response, but she had neither the will nor the strength to act otherwise at the time.

Now she wanted to retaliate, to hurt him as

cruelly as he had hurt her. She stared up at him with a tremendous feeling of loss. Then, with all the contempt she could muster, she said, 'I know you will find it difficult to understand because you believe you are always right, but I do *not* fancy the idea of going to bed with you at all. I'm sorry if you are disappointed.'

He flushed a dark, angry red. 'As you are usually so liberal with your—favours—may I ask what has changed your attitude?'

At his words and his tone of voice she felt a flash of real hatred. In the sweetest, most reasonable of voices, she said, 'Well you see, Miles, I need to fancy the man, and—I'm awfully sorry to be so blunt—I don't fancy you at all.'

He was bewildered and deeply hurt and angry. He felt certain she was not speaking the truth. But why? Had he been wrong about her? Had he blatantly insulted her by the things he had said and thereby lost even her friendly companionship?

'Get your coat on and I will take you back,' he said in a quiet, efficient voice.

Her throat tightened. So this was the end of everything. There would be no more pleasant outings with him, no promised weekend at his mother's home. In future, instead of looking forward each day to seeing him in the hospital she would have to try and avoid him. The merest glimpse of him had always brightened the dullest day, now there would be nothing.

She sat beside him in the car, as far away from him as she could get. If she had dared to glance at his face she would have seen that he looked as unhappy as she felt. They were silent until the nurses' hostel came in sight, then he stopped the car and leaning across her opened the door.

'I'll drop you here,' he said.

She was surprised that he did not take her to her door. Then she understood. It was in case anyone saw them together so late at night. He was not worried about her reputation but about his own. And in case word of it got to Sister Bell's ears.

'Thank you,' she murmured politely, as she tried to steady her trembling lips.

'Goodnight.'

He waited until she was safely inside before driving away.

No sooner had she gone through the door of the hostel than the tears which she had been holding back rained down her cheeks. Covering her face with her hands, and trying to check her sobs, she ran blindly up the stairs to her room.

CHAPTER ELEVEN

HELENA HAD spent a completely sleepless night. She could never forget the thrill of Miles's kisses, or the way in which her body, with a volition of its own, had responded to them. She relived the ecstasy, the feeling that her bones had melted in the fire of her love. She knew she could have experienced the most utter bliss if she had agreed to do what he asked and spend the night with him. Was she quite mad to have refused?

She realised that it would have been the briefest of brief affairs but the future could hold nothing else so magical and sexually the past was empty, for she was a virgin. Was it naive of her in these days to value that and wish to remain that way until she met the man who would be her husband?

She knew that was not entirely the reason she had refused him. It was mostly because of his changed attitude, the feeling that he was slightly contemptuous of her, as if he believed he need only make the suggestion to have her eagerly agree. Had he said that he loved her the outcome would have been different, but he was too honourable a man to lie about a thing like that. Lucky, lucky Sister Bell to be able to share his passion—*and* his love.

A weight pressed against her heart and gave her a feeling of desolation. Why, oh why had she said such cruel things to him? He had not lied to her, so why had she lied to him? Not fancy him? Oh God! how untrue that was. How deeply she must have hurt his pride. Apart from that moment of anger, she would not have hurt him for anything in the world. It was true that he had hurt her too, but he had more reason. He had obviously believed she was having an affair with Bill, and maybe others, and she had done nothing to refute that. On the contrary she may have encouraged him in that belief.

She thought with dismay of the future. It was almost inevitable that she would meet Mrs Tracy again at Aunt Norah's, and Miles would be her chauffeur. She couldn't sit beside him and talk naturally to him after what had happened, and Aunt Norah was perceptive enough to know that something was amiss. Yet she had to continue spending her spare time at Stipplewick or life would not be worth living, especially now that she could not look forward happily to Miles's visits to the ward.

She moved from side to side, her mind weary with going over and over the happenings of the previous day. There were the sounds of the hospital coming to life, cars and lorries making their deliveries and collections, an ambulance setting out smoothly and swiftly on call and nearby the slam of bedroom doors and water running for baths. Helena's eyes were gritty with lack of sleep but she dared not close them in case she dozed off.

She flung back the bedclothes with a smothered groan and got out of bed. Then, gathering together her clothes, she padded across the landing to the shower room. Feeling marginally brighter, she set off for the dining-room across the garden, glad that for once she had the time to do so, for it was good to smell the freshness of the air. Later in the day it seemed more used up, past its prime.

She was earlier than usual and neither Collins nor Coe had yet arrived in the dining-room. For once Helena was glad. Her toast went around and around in her mouth, seeming to increase in bulk like meat in a mincer and she had difficulty in swallowing it. She saw Bill arrive and go to the counter. Leaving what was left of her breakfast she slipped out before he could notice her. Quite unreasonably she blamed him for most of her troubles.

Nurse Lester was back on duty and Helena joined her in the linen room.

'Hello, you've been on weekend leave I suppose?' Nurse Lester folded blankets and placed them in a neat pile.

'Yes, and before that you were on sick leave, so I haven't seen you for ages. Are you better?'

'Yes thanks. Mind you, I felt pretty rotten, I don't often go sick. Now my husband has caught the bug. Still, he isn't as ill as he thinks he is.' She reached up for a blanket on a high shelf. 'Do you know that we've got Mrs Plumley back with us?'

'Mrs Plumley?' Helena repeated in disbelief.

Nurse Lester chuckled. 'I thought that would shake you.'

'It's done that all right. Why has she come back? What's wrong with her?'

'What she came in for the first time.'

'But her tests proved negative.'

'Most of them. But not the final one.'

Helena hugged a sheet to her chest. 'Oh no! The poor woman. What a terrible thing to happen.'

'Mmm. Almost worse than if she'd been told it was malignant in the first place. Chuck over those other blankets, will you?'

'Why was she discharged before all the tests had been made?'

Nurse Lester added another folded blanket to the growing pile. 'Search me,' she said.

'It's—it's unbelievable. Dreadful.'

'I've never known it to happen before. I suppose it was due to the shortage of beds. As everything seemed to be OK they didn't want to keep a bed occupied unnecessarily.'

'How has she taken it? You couldn't blame her, whatever sort of a mood she was in. I can't think of anything worse.'

Nurse Lester's shiny face looked puzzled. 'They say there's nowt so queer as folk and it's true. Would you believe she's been as good as gold and no trouble at all?'

'I daresay she's suffering from shock. I know I should be.'

'You may be right. Then heaven help us when she recovers from that!'

Helena counted the pillowcases and made a note of them.

'She threatened to complain to the hospital board about getting the wrong flowers, so what is she going to do about this?'

'Thank goodness that isn't our problem.'

Helena stood up on a stool to check the top shelves. 'What's happened to all the draw-sheets? We're right down on them. Do you reckon patients take them home with them?'

'That wouldn't surprise me. But we'll be getting a supply from the laundry now the unpleasantness is over.'

'Oh yes, of course. That's going to upset our list, isn't it? We will appear to be short on everything.'

'I'll add a note to that effect,' Nurse Lester said.

'Who is to blame about Mrs Plumley?' Helena asked.

Nurse Lester chuckled maliciously. 'Surprise, surprise! I think it is our wonder-man who may have boobed.'

Helena's body gave a sudden twitch. 'You mean Mr Tracy?'

'Who else? He must have said she was in the clear.'

'And that she could be discharged?'

'No, that would be Sister Bell. But those two will stick together, never fear.'

After a few minutes Helena said, 'Are they—are they still—I can't say I've ever seen them together. I mean off duty.'

'What do you expect? They keep that sort of thing very much under their hats, you may depend on that. They can't have a word of gossip about our chief consultant.'

'No gossip?' Helena protested. 'I've heard nothing but gossip about them since I came here.'

'Ah, but that is educated surmise, we have no actual proof—or didn't have. But when I was passing Sister's door just now it was slightly open and I glanced in and there they were, snogging.'

Helena stared at her, wanting desperately to disbelieve her.

'With the door open?'

'Ah, that's boob number two,' Nurse Lester laughed. 'Love can make even the best of us slip up, it seems.'

Helena made no reply but jotted down the final number of sheets and pretended to have difficulty with the totting up. Her heart was like a ball of lead inside her.

'Righto, that's this little lot done. Now for the medicine round.'

Helena followed her to the landing where she unlocked the trolley.

When they came to Miss Hobbs' bed Helena queried the fact that she was still there.

'Hello Miss Hobbs, everything all right?' Without waiting for her answer, Nurse Lester said in an undertone to Helena, 'No, they believe she collapsed rather than tripped up. But she's getting on all right. It'll take time, of course. They're running tests on her.'

A young woman now occupied the bed that had been Mrs Coley's.

'What is she in for?' Helena asked.

'Two pills for Miss Ashford,' Nurse Lester said, handing the small tray on which they were placed to Helena.

When she returned, Nurse Lester said with a snort, 'You may well ask why that young madam is in here. I don't know what this country is coming to. People may have been a bit too narrow-minded in my day but that was preferable to what it's like nowadays.'

'Why? Is she unmarried and pregnant?'

'She was. Yesterday she had her pregnancy terminated.'

'Well, that's not unusual. Sometimes it can be the best decision, I suppose.'

'Sometimes it can. But there she is, not much more than a child, and she was sterilised at the same time. I know it isn't our function to moralise and, goodness knows, I try not to, but at times like this I find it very difficult.'

Helena's eyes darkened sympathetically. 'Poor kid, there must have been some very good reason.'

'If so they've kept it a secret. All I know is what I've told you.'

When the medicine round was finished and the trolley locked away, two patients were prepared for X-ray.

'The physiotherapist said I was to go to the gym for exercises for my leg,' Miss Ashford said. 'I don't want to miss out, I want to be fit to go skiing in a couple of months' time. My boyfriend has booked for us to go to Switzerland.'

Helena rang down to the gym, then arranged for Nurse Jelbart to accompany her down there.

'Mrs Dugdale, you are to have a bath, so if you'll get your things together I'll take you along to the bathroom.'

Helena held her arm as they walked slowly and carefully across the ward. As they neared the doors they opened and Sister Bell and Mr Tracy came through. Helena's heart lurched and momentarily she felt in need of Mrs Dugdale's support rather than the other way round. Her eyes blurred, but when they cleared she felt stricken at the distant expression on his face, the blank look of non-recognition.

When they had passed she heard him murmur something and then they both laughed. She knew quite well that they were not laughing at her, they would neither of them consider her to be of sufficient importance to even mention, but she felt excluded; her eyes stung and she had an over-whelming longing to lie down and weep as if she had suffered a great loss.

She dealt with Mrs Dugdale's needs and answered her questions automatically. When they returned to the ward and she had settled her patient in bed she joined Bill, who was at Miss Hobbs's bedside. There was an anxious look on the old lady's face as she pleated the edge of her sheet nervously.

'But I can't understand why I collapsed, Doctor, I've never done such a thing before. I hope there's nothing seriously wrong?'

He smiled at her reassuringly. 'No Miss Hobbs, there is nothing at all for you to worry about. As we get older there are any number of minor things that can cause a dizzy spell—even wax in the ears! Now, if it had happened in your bedroom you would have forgotten almost immediately. But you chose to fall against a granite headstone and that was not a very good idea, was it?' He squeezed her shoulder. 'All the tests so far have proved satisfactory but we have a few more to make. But not to worry, we are very happy with your condition.'

She gave him a relieved smile. 'Thank you, Doctor, that's taken a load off my mind. I can't afford to be ill, you see, because I live by myself.'

As they walked away, Helena asked Bill if he had any other patients he wanted her to see with him.

'Yes please. That kid over there.'

Helena followed his glance. 'Isn't she the one who has been sterilised?'

'She is indeed,' he said, his lips tightening.

'But why, Bill? I think that is terribly sad at her age.'

He nodded. 'There are medical reasons for the decision with which I cannot argue. But what gets me is her attitude.'

'You mean she can't come to terms with it? But you can understand that, at her age.'

'I mean nothing of the kind. You would have thought she had just heard she had won the pools when she was told the op had been carried out.'

Helena looked dubious. 'Isn't that better than being terribly upset? That would be heart-breaking.'

Bill raised his shoulders. 'That's very true. But more natural.'

They stopped at the girl's bedside. 'Hello, Sharon, how are you today?' he asked.

The girl in her revealing nylon nightdress sat up in bed, her hair an untidy tangle over her head.

'Great. I'm feeling great, Doctor.'

Bill looked so severe that Helena could scarcely

recognise him as the seemingly carefree jolly young man she knew.

'Good. No pain?'

The girl looked at him consideringly. 'Yes, I do have a pain. A bad pain.'

Bill hesitated. Then he glanced at Helena and back to Sharon.

'Then I had better take a look. Nurse, curtains please.'

Helena drew the curtains and arranged the sheet to expose only the area he needed to examine. Sharon pushed the sheet aside and drew up her nightdress.

'It's not there, it's here.'

Bill put the sheet back again and prodded her gently with his expert fingers.

Sharon was clearly in no great distress but gazed boldly at him from over made-up eyes. She gestured towards Helena.

'What did you bring her with you for? Are you scared or something?'

Bill continued with his examination. 'Everything seems satisfactory. It is natural to have a little pain. Right. You can pull back the curtains, Nurse.' He covered her with the rest of the bedclothes.

Sharon moved some chewing gum from one side of her mouth to the other. 'You wouldn't be a bad-looking bloke if you was dressed proper. Or undressed,' she said with a loud laugh. Then she shot Helena a dark look. 'Where'd she come from? Out the museum?'

'I think you are trying to shock us, aren't you, Sharon? Now you be a good girl,' he said pleasantly. 'I will look in on you again tomorrow.'

'Bet you a quid you won't come alone,' she said.

'You're dead right, I won't,' Bill replied, and they all laughed.

'Have you got any more patients to see?' Helena asked as they walked away.

'Not in this ward.'

Helena followed him into the corridor. 'What a girl,' she said with a laugh.

'Sharon? She was on her best behaviour this morning. A result of you being there.'

'Me? The museum piece?'

'How unkind of her,' he said with a laugh and laid an arm around her shoulders.

Sister Bell's door opened. Miles came out and Bill's arm felt like a ton weight on Helena's shoulders. He gazed at them both coldly before Bill moved away.

Sister Bell said sharply, 'Nurse Chamberlain, if you have nothing better to do than gossip in the corridor I can find you plenty of work. Check the CSSD supplies and make out the stock level sheets, please.'

'But, Sister, I was on my way to fetch a bedpan,' Helena explained.

'Then I should imagine your patient no longer has need for it and her bed will probably need changing.'

'Yes, Sister,' Helena mumbled.

And I will want the stock level sheets.'

'If I have time, Sister.'

Sister Bell seemed to grow an inch taller. '*If* you have time? You will *make* time, Nurse. If necessary you will do them in your meal break.'

'Yes, Sister.' Helena was painfully conscious of Miles's presence as he gazed over her head while waiting for Sister Bell to accompany him.

She fetched a bedpan and took it to Mrs Wood, who was suffering from acute cystitis and seemd to require one permanently.

'Mrs Wood?' She gave a questioning smile.

'Bless you, Nurse, you must be a mind-reader, I was just going to ring for one.'

Helena went over to Mrs Plumley reluctantly.

'So you are back with us again,' she said, making a pretence of reading her notes.

There were no hot-house blooms on her bedside table this time. She was wearing the expensive nightdress and matching bedjacket that she had worn before, but the expression on her face was different. There was none of the petulance, just a look of subdued acceptance. She looked doubtfully at Helena.

'I don't suppose you are too pleased to see me again, Nurse, and I can't blame you.'

Helena gave a look of friendly concern. 'Naturally I am sorry you have had to come back. How are you feeling?'

She shook her head. 'Numb, Nurse, numb.'

'I should think so.'

'It's a funny thing. Last time I hardly knew what I was doing or saying. I was a bundle of nerves, wanted to hit out at everybody. It had happened so quickly you see, I hadn't time to adjust.'

'No, but that's the way it is. Doctors like to check these things straight away and waste no time. You and the doctors did all that was possible—it's just a shame it has turned out this way.'

Mrs Plumley looked thoughtful. 'I don't know what's got into me, I seem to have got strength from somewhere. I feel that what is to be will be.'

'I'm so glad. It's wonderful to be able to feel like that about it, and so very sensible.'

Mrs Plumley continued speaking as if she had learned the words by heart. 'I'm sixty-nine and I have never been in hospital before, so I feel I can't really grumble. Some people suffer so long.'

Helena could think of nothing to say. The stock phrases were not applicable. She squeezed Mrs Plumley's hand and determined that when she had the time she would go to the stall opposite the hospital and buy her some flowers.

She was kept too busy to dwell on her own affairs and compared with the problems some of the patients were facing Helena realised they were trivial. But she could still see the cold expression on Miles's face when he saw Bill with his arm around her. Undoubtedly he would think they had been talking of personal matters. She could still feel the embarrassment of knowing he was there when Sister Bell reprimanded her. But what did it matter? His opinion of her was already so low nothing in the future could make any difference and she must try to be resigned to that.

Helena managed to get the stock level sheets done, but the extra work encroached on her meal break. She unpinned her apron and hurried to the dining-room, but on seeing the queue of nurses waiting for a hot meal decided to get some soup and a sandwich to save time.

She hurried back to the hospital by the covered way, dodging in and out between nurses going to and from the dining-room. The lift seemed to take for ever before it arrived. Helena dashed out and pinned on her apron in record time and was hoping to slip into the ward without being noticed, but Nurse Lester was standing near the doors glaring at her watch.

'I was thinking you'd gone on leave again. You should have relieved me seven minutes ago.'

'Is it so long? I'm very sorry, I got held up.'

'Now I'll have a long wait in the queue,' she grumbled, pushing some papers into Helena's hands. 'There's a new admission arrived. I've done nothing about her because I was expecting you back, so you'd better see to her right away.'

Helena went across to the middle-aged woman wearing a tweed coat and beret who was standing beside a blue suitcase and looking as if she had missed the last bus for the day.

'Hello.' Helena glanced down at the forms Nurse Lester had given her. 'Mrs Ford—is that right? Well, if you'll come along with me I'll get you settled.'

She led the way to a bed which had been prepared earlier in the day, then drew the curtains around it.

'Here we are, Mrs Ford. Now, if you will get undressed and pop into bed I'll be back again in a few minutes. All right?'

When she had dealt with the calls of other patients she returned to the newcomer.

'That's right. Have you taken everything you need from your case? I will take it outside and perhaps one of your visitors will take it home for you next time they come—we are rather pushed for space. Your towel goes on this rack and your slippers in the bottom of your locker. Sister will create if she sees them under the bed, they look untidy and get in the way of the cleaners. I should have your dressing-gown handy. Tea will be coming around in about half an hour. Have you brought in something to read?' She reeled off all the necessary information.

The woman shook her head. 'No, Nurse, I didn't think of it. I was so busy leaving things right for the family. I wish I had.'

'Would you like me to borrow something for you to read? Because the library won't be in again today.'

'Thank you very much, that would be nice.'

Helena walked over to Miss Carter, who had a pile of magazines on her bedside table.

'Would you be a dear and lend a couple of these to the new patient, please?'

Miss Carter gave an expansive smile. 'Certainly, dear, take what you like, only leave me the top few. I'm in the middle of one of the serials. My word! The trouble the poor soul is in. And it's true, too, it says so on the cover. I'm thankful I'm not in such a pickle. Not that I'm likely to have two men fancying me at the same time!' She gave a loud laugh.

'Where are your dentures, Miss Carter?' Helena asked as she selected a couple of magazines.

'In my locker, dear. I can't get on with them, they hurt my poor gums.'

'I think you should try to wear them. Sister Bell will be cross if you don't. She is very particular about that.'

Helena found them and handed them to her. 'Wear them a little longer each day and you may get used to them. Thanks for the magazines. I'll see that you get them back.'

'Don't bother, dear, I've finished with them, I've read them all. Well, here goes.' She put in her dentures and gnashed them together. Then she gave a horrible smile. 'Do you reckon they make me look sexy? They should do, they're agony.'

Teas were given out and then cleared away before Helena had a chance to go to Sister Bell's office. She knocked tentatively on the door.

'Come in.'

Helena took a deep breath and went inside. Sister Bell continued writing. After some moments she glanced up. Looking as if she did not much care for what she saw, she said, 'Oh it's you, Nurse. What is it now?'

'The stock level sheets, Sister.' Helena handed them over.

'Oh yes. Thank you.' She glanced at them, then looked up with a serious expression on her face.

'I am not happy at depriving you of your break time, Nurse. You work hard and need the rest, I understand that perfectly. But increasingly it seems that it takes more than a verbal reprimand to remind you of our rules. You know that gossiping in the corridors is not allowed, and when it comes to chatting with a doctor, and one of Mr Tracy's team, you are really stretching our patience to the limit.'

'Yes, Sister. I'm sorry, Sister.'

'Hm, so you say. But I am not at all sure that I won't catch you doing it again. Maybe our standards are different from those at St Ann's, but you are working here now and the sooner you conform to our ways the better it will be for all concerned. We are all getting a little tired of your constant lapses.'

'Yes, Sister,' Helena murmured.

Sister Bell gave her a rather sweet smile. 'But your record is not all bad, Nurse. I understand the patients like you and when all is said and done that is a very important factor. Apparently you are kind and caring. So cheer up, Nurse. You may go.'

Helena thanked her and left with a sudden surge of happiness. But her happiness was on the surface. Her heart was heavy. In every contact she had with Miles she appeared in a bad light and he made it quite obvious that he despised her. That being the case, she wondered why he had asked her to spend the night with him. If she had done so might his attitude towards her have improved? Or would he have despised her even more?

She wondered with a wry smile what Sister Bell's reaction would be if she knew of his invitation to her. The smile faded as a wave of hurt pride enveloped her. How dared he treat her as if she was nothing more than a push-over? 'Nobody will be any the wiser' he had said. And with those words she believed he had killed her love for him.

CHAPTER TWELVE

HELENA TOOK her breakfast tray to an empty table in the hope that she could be alone long enough to read the letter from her mother. She took a sip of her coffee, then tore open the envelope. Her mother's bold handwriting was easy to read. After thanking her for her letter and giving news of their health she wrote about their growing fascination with their new country—the bazaars and exotic lifestyle . . .

It seems a pity for you not to take advantage of our being here to come out for a couple of years. The hospitals are out of this world, with marvellous equipment, so I'm told. Promise to think about it . . .

Helena stopped reading as she buttered her toast. For the first time the idea of joining her parents appealed to her, for Trelawny had lost its charm and going to Stipplewick presented problems.

Tomorrow was the start of her short weekend off duty and she did not view the prospect happily. She was scared that the Tracys might come over, for it was only a few miles drive and Emily and Norah were obviously soul-mates. That would be fine, she had no objection to that, it was Emily's chauffeur who worried her. What would she do when she saw him? What could they talk about? They were civilised and would be polite to one another, but for all those hours when Emily and Norah had time for nobody but each other? She shuddered. It would be dreadful.

'You look as if you've given away a twenty pence piece instead of a fivepenny one.' Collins noticed the open letter. 'Oh, sorry. I hope it isn't bad news?'

Helena folded it and put it back in the envelope. 'No, anything but. My mother is trying to persuade me to take a job in Kuwait for a couple of years. I suppose I should, really. One should see as much of the world as one can and this is an excellent opportunity.'

'I suppose so. But Kuwait? I can't say it appeals to me. All that heat! All those men in their white robes floating around like ghosts. No, I wouldn't move away from here. Besides, you haven't been here five minutes. Is it your aunt's match-making that's getting you down?'

'No. No, she seems to have taken the hint over that. But—I don't know, I just feel fed-up.'

'Don't we all at times? When is your next free spell?'

'Tomorrow for the weekend.'

'Lucky you. You'll feel a new person after that. Are you going by bike?'

'No, I'm not busting a gut to get there. I'll go by bus.'

After a moment Collins said, 'Coe is in the seventh heaven at the moment.'

'Why? What's happened to her?'

'It's Bill. You know she's had a thing about

him—well lots of us have—but she more than most. Twice this week he's taken her out—as opposed to in. Once to a meal and once to a sort of nightclub near Redruth!'

'Heavens, what does he use for money?' Helena asked, knowing how hard-up young doctors usually were.

'He gets an allowance from his parents. They live in a huge house near Camborne. She's hoping he will take her there. I'll believe it when it happens.'

'I hope it works out for her. I like Bill a lot, he's good fun.'

'Yes, I'm fond of him too, but I don't think I could ever take him seriously. He's had too many girls for my liking.'

'So he's sown his wild oats. Maybe he's ready to settle down.'

'That type never settles down. He might get married but I wouldn't bet on him remaining faithful.'

'Would you bet on any man doing that?'

Collins laughed. 'You *are* in a mood! On your bike, back to work in case it's infectious.'

Some of the patients had left and new ones had taken their place. Miss Hobbs had been sent to a convalescent home near where a cousin lived. Sharon had been fetched by a shy young man who clearly adored her. Helena wondered whether his parents were heart-broken at his choice of girlfriend.

She went across to Mrs Plumley, who had now had her operation.

'How are you today?' Helena straightened her bedding.

'Surprisingly well, thank you. They're coming to measure me up for a bra.' She smiled. 'Mr Tracy has assured me that I will still have my sex appeal.'

Helena joined in her laughter. 'That's nice to know! I suppose you will soon be leaving us?'

'Yes, any day now. But I will have to come back to Outpatients.'

'Then you must pop up here and let us know how you are getting on.'

Sister Bell and Mr Tracy came into the ward looking very pleased with themselves and continued their animated conversation before starting their round. Their happiness seemed contagious and all the patients perked up after their visit, which was completed quicker than usual.

'We'll do the medicine round now, Nurse.' Nurse Lester fetched the trolley. The usual ritual had begun. When they had completed the round they went to the kitchen.

'Coffee or tea?' Helena asked.

'The new coffee-bags are quite good, we'll have those, shall we?'

They sat on stools and thankfully sipped their hot drink. Nurse Lester said, 'So it's all excitement today.'

Helena looked puzzled. 'Is it?'

'Didn't you notice Mr Tracy and Sister Bell?'

'I—I thought they seemed very pleased with themselves—why?'

'My dear, haven't you looked at the notice-board?'

Helena shook her head. 'No, I never do.'

'Well it's time you did. Go and take a look.'

'No—you tell me.'

The telephone rang in Sister Bell's office. Nurse Lester rose to her feet. 'Sister isn't there, I'll have to answer it.'

Helena finished her coffee then rinsed out the cups. Curiosity made her take the lift to the ground floor to look at the staff notice board. There was information regarding meetings and lectures, items for sale, tickets available for an organ recital and several other things, but nothing to warrant any excitement she would have thought. Then, as she was about to walk away, she caught sight of a card.

Friday, 7 p.m. Senior Consultant's room. Members of staff are cordially invited to toast Sister Bell's future happiness.

Helena stretched out a hand to steady herself as the notice-board seemed to slither around in front of her. It was some moments before she felt able to return to the ward. She carried out her duties like an automaton, speaking to the patients, joking with them, but anyone gazing into her eyes would have seen in them a stricken look.

She had known that one day this would happen, of course. She had been warned that Sister Bell was at the top of Mr Tracy's list, but that knowledge could not ease the ache in her heart or lessen her feeling of loss. She knew that it would be impossible to go on working here when Miles actually belonged to someone else. It would be immoral to picture herself in his arms, to dream of the bliss of his kisses, to sometimes long for the clock to be turned back so that she could once again be asked to spend the night with him and possibly come to a different conclusion.

She was certain that no man whom she might meet in the future could instil in her such passionate longing or fascinate her as he did with his tone of voice, physique and half-hidden eyes. She could picture him before her always, whether she was in the hospital, on a country road, or in her room.

Had she been an artist she could have made an exact drawing of him. She knew every line on his face, every silver-tipped hair, and the angle of the little V-shaped scar on his left cheek. She had to admit to herself that she loved him with her every breath. But her feelings were ambivalent, for at times she hated him. But the hatred was born of her love and was a part of it.

Nurse Lester came to her with a list in her hand. 'You've seen the notice? So let's have your quid if you can afford it. I've been given the job of collecting for a wedding present.'

'Wh—what are you getting?'

'She's asked for a double duvet. I suppose she's had her fill of making beds in the past.'

Helena fetched her purse and handed over the note. 'When are you going to buy it?'

'I can't get it before tonight, that's certain. They didn't give us much notice, did they? Maybe they wanted to make it official after I caught them kissing. I wonder if we'll have sherry or champagne? I should think Mr Tracy could afford to splash out on champagne.'

'Then the patients will be in for a merry time with

the staff half sozzled,' Helena said, forcing herself
to speak lightly.

'Thank goodness we will be off duty. Shall we go
down together?'

Everything in Helena rebelled at the idea. She
could not drink to their happiness although she
wished them well. She could not bear to hear their
names coupled or possibly see them kiss as they
accepted congratulations.

'I shan't be going, I'm afraid. I've decided to go
to Stipplewick tonight instead of waiting for the
morning.'

There was a knowing look in Nurse Lester's eyes
as they glinted behind her glasses. 'What made you
change your mind?'

Helena shrugged. 'It seemed a pity not to make it
as long a weekend as possible.'

That was partly the reason, for now she knew
that she need not fear that Miles would arrive on
her aunt's doorstep. He would be with Sister Bell.
She wondered whether she lived locally and pictured the pleasure of her family, if she had one,
when they heard the news. Lucky, lucky Sister Bell
who had everything—looks, prestige, brains and
Miles Tracy.

When she was off duty and back in her room
Helena took out her mother's letter and read it
again. It had come at the right moment. At any
other time the suggestion that she might go to
Kuwait would have made no impression on her at
all, but now it seemed the solution. She need not
wait until a vacancy occurred in a Kuwaiti hospital,
for it really would not matter if she worked or not.

Many people took a year or two off work to travel, to take stock of life and themselves. If a vacancy cropped up she would be on the spot to apply for it. It was a splendid idea—so why did she fling herself on the bed and bury her face in her pillow and feel the trickle of tears on her cheeks? Oh Miles, Miles, I do love you so, she said silently.

It would soon be dark and she did not fancy cycling to Stipplewick, but it was a lot better than going to the chief consultant's room to have a congratulatory drink and to pretend pleasure. She changed quickly into jeans and a sweater and set off on the journey before she could spend too long disliking the idea.

Fortunately the roads were practically deserted. The lanes were unlit and very dark because of the dense foliage. As she cycled past a gate which led into a field she discerned the figure of a man leaning against the top bar and her heart leapt. She pedalled furiously, and when she had to dismount to climb a hill she was breathless and too scared to look back over her shoulder.

It was with a feeling of immense relief that she reached the green and saw the light in Aunt Norah's widow. Only then did she remember that she had not phoned her to say that she would be arriving.

She rang the bell and Rocky set up a furious barking. After a minute Aunt Norah opened the door and looked out.

'Helena, it's you! I didn't expect you until the morning. The side is open so put your bike around the back and I'll let you in through the kitchen.'

It was good to sit in the warm, well-lit room with a cup of tea and a slice of her aunt's fruit cake. This was the atmosphere which she much preferred to the thought of an air-conditioned house in the hot climate of Kuwait on the edge of the desert where the only people she would know were her parents. But she must make that move.

Later in the evening Helena read extracts of the letter to her aunt.

'So I was thinking it would be a good idea for me to join them. I'd never get such an opportunity again to see that part of the world.'

Aunt Norah put down her knitting. 'Surely you are not seriously considering doing that? I thought you liked it at Trelawny.'

'I do! Or rather, I did. I—I can't stay there now.'

'What do you mean? Why can't you?'

Helena stared into the fire. There was no need for her to keep quiet about her secret any longer and she wanted so much to speak to somebody about it.

'He—he's engaged. He got engaged today,' she said bleakly.

'Just a minute. Who are we talking about?'

Helena's eyes opened wide. 'Why—the doctor I told you about.'

'Oh him! Well never mind, love, you'll get over that. And you did know all along that he wasn't for you, didn't you? That's what you said.'

'But now it's a fact and that makes all the difference. I can't stay on there now, seeing him every day coming into the ward, loving him, knowing that he belongs to somebody else.'

'You can, of course you can. You'll meet someone else, you mark my words.'

Helena sighed. Nobody would ever understand
her feelings. She doubted whether she would have
taken anyone else seriously if they had admitted
such deep love for someone who had been no more
than the merest acquaintance.

'What about that—that person from St Ives?'

'You mean Bob?' She shook her head. 'I was
never serious about him.'

'Thank heavens for that.' Aunt Norah thought
for a minute. 'Well now, what about Emily's son?
I'm sure you'd go a long way to meet a nicer man
than Miles. And I think he likes you.'

'He doesn't. Of course he doesn't.'

'I'm not so sure.'

'Well you're wrong because—oh, Aunt Norah,
he got engaged to Sister Bell today,' she wailed.

'*Both* of them got engaged?' Aunt Norah
frowned.

'Of course. It takes two . . .'

'No, I mean both doctors? You said the one
you—don't tell me I had it wrong! It isn't Miles
you're in love with, is it?'

'It is, of course it is,' Helena whispered, and felt a
great surge of relief that she could voice it. For so
long it had been hidden inside her.

'Well, my dear, I don't know what I can say.
There's not a lot we can do about that, is there? I'm
surprised at Emily, she never mentioned a word.
You would have thought she would have said
something.'

'She probably didn't know. I remember she said

that he kept his private affairs to himself.'

'So she did. Well then, she's got a surprise coming to her.'

'So you do see, don't you, that I can't stay down here? Not only would I be seeing him in the hospital but—so much worse—I'd be meeting him here. And I can't *do* that, Aunt Norah, I really can't.'

'Well, I don't know what to say. I can sympathise with your feelings up to a point—I know you won't believe me when I tell you that you will get over it. But leaving the hospital, giving up a good job and going half across the world seems a very drastic solution. You are not likely to meet anyone over there to take your mind off him.'

Helena slowly shook her head. 'I don't want to meet anyone else and I don't want to forget him. But I must get away. Later on I'll carry on nursing and maybe do what you did, go on the district.'

Aunt Norah sighed. 'I've always suspected that you laughed at my match-making, but I've never got mix-ups like this, they always work out fine.'

When Helena awoke in the morning she felt quite determined. She would join her parents as soon as possible. She only needed to give two weeks' notice at the hospital.

There was a tap on her door and her aunt came in with tea and sat on the end of her bed.

'It's a real treat to be waited on. I can't remember being given early morning tea in bed before,' Helena said. 'Couldn't you sleep?'

'I had a telephone call.'

'Wrong number? Who would ring so early?'

'It was Emily.'

Helena spilt some tea. 'She—they aren't coming over?'

Her aunt nodded. 'I'm afraid they are. I suppose it is to tell me their news.'

'I can't see him, I can't,' Helena cried.

'Well no, I understand, and I've been thinking about that. Why not take Rocky for a long walk and have lunch out somewhere? There are one or two places in the square. There's The Turk's Head, that's quite nice.'

Helena nodded. 'Yes, I'll do that. You do understand, don't you? You don't think I'm being stupid?'

'Of course I don't.' She patted her shoulder. 'I'm about to make breakfast, so up you get.'

'What time are they arriving, did they say?'

'About eleven o'clock.'

'So I'll have to be out for a long time. Where can I take Rocky for all that time?'

'Let me see.' Aunt Norah thought for a minute. 'Bluebell Dell is one of his favourite places, and he can have a good run without you having to bother about him. You turn left down a lane beside the church. It leads you eventually through fields and more lanes out on to the main road. There are several big boulders you can take a rest on, they'll be quite dry.'

'Does the main road lead on into the square?'

'No, you'll have to turn back and retrace your steps.'

Helena wore no make-up and didn't need any. Her eyes looked dark blue against her pale golden tan and her lips were naturally pink. Her apricot shirt, open at the neck and worn over beige trousers, complemented her colouring, for the lengthy hot spell had bleached her hair to a light brown.

Rocky pranced beside her, straining in every direction until they were clear of the square and he could be taken off his lead. The fields were on the hillside and all around were miles of gorse and heather, the flowers burnt brown now after weeks of unseasonable sunshine. There was open country for as far as one could see, blue-rimmed by the sea.

Gulls circled overhead, squawking with delight as they swooped down to savour some fish manure which the farmer had put on his fields. Black and white cows were grazing in a far corner and Helena hoped that Rocky would not tease them. The paths were steeper than they looked and eventually Helena decided to take a rest while Rocky ran delightedly to and fro.

She closed her eyes in the warm sunlight and breathed in the soft, sweet air and thought how peaceful it was. Apart from Rocky. Heavens! She hoped he was not chasing the cows.

'Rocky, stop that noise,' she called, but he continued barking.

She opened her eyes reluctantly to see what he was doing and saw him racing towards a lone figure. She gave a gasp as she saw who it was.

Miles strode the last few yards until he reached her boulder, then sat down beside her.

'Why—why have you come here?'

'To find you,' he said simply. 'Aunt Norah told me where you would be.'

'Aunt Norah? Oh no! What did you want me for?'

He took her hand in his strong, firm grasp. 'To clear up a few misunderstandings. Firstly, I am *not* engaged to Sister Bell—or to anyone else.'

'But—I read it on the notice-board. You put it there.'

He shook his head. 'No. What you read there was that I invited staff to my consulting room to drink Sister Bell's happiness. As chief consultant I would do that for any senior member of staff who was about to get married.'

A weight which had seemed a part of her suddenly disappeared. 'You mean—you aren't—she isn't?'

'I mean that she is getting married to the consultant whom I replaced. It isn't hospital policy to allow an engaged couple to work together, so he moved away. They are now getting married.'

Helena's brain whirled. 'But everybody assumed . . .'

'I have no doubt they did.'

'And—and someone saw you kissing her.'

He laughed ironically. 'Staff Nurse Lester! I thought she would put that around. It was a kiss of friendly congratulations. Had it been more than that I would have made sure that the door was shut.'

'Kisses are not always what they seem,' she said slowly.

He looked at her thoughtfully. 'You mean—you and Bill? Was I wrong about that?'

She nodded. 'He had a party and I stayed behind

to wash the dishes because the others were on duty. He kissed me goodnight.' She flashed him an accusing glance. 'Had it been more than that he would no doubt have made sure that the door was shut, don't you think?'

A feeling of tremendous relief washed over him. 'And what about the man in Stipplewick square?'

'That was Bob, and it meant nothing at all. He was rehearsing a part for the benefit of Aunt Norah.'

'Aunt Norah? Tell me more.'

'It's a long story.'

'I've got all the time in the world.'

Helena searched for the right words. 'You see, she is anxious for me to get married—so to put her off I asked Bob, who is just a casual acquaintance from London, to pretend to be my fiancé. He took some persuading.'

'He didn't appear to be very reluctant when I saw him.'

'But he was. It was only when I threatened him that he couldn't stay for lunch that he kissed me— to prove that he could act the part.'

There was a faint smile in his eyes. 'And to think I was so angry—so jealous—'

Her eyes widened. 'You were jealous of Bob? Of me? But I was nothing to you.'

'Do you really believe that?'

'Y—yes. Whenever I came into contact with you you were always so angry with me.'

'You must remember that first and foremost I am a doctor, Helena. If anybody does anything which could harm my patients or anybody or anything I am responsible for, I am angry. If necessary I would get that person dismissed, whoever it was. But I am also a man. Even when I was extremely angry with you, I loved you. I loved everything about you.'

The words which sounded so wonderful did not ring true. She shook her head vehemently. 'No, you didn't, you couldn't have done. When you— you asked me to—to stay at your flat . . . ' The colour flooded her cheeks. 'You didn't love me then. You desired me, we desired each other, but you also despised me, I could tell.'

He stared out over the acres of rusty bracken to the sea.

'Yes, I did despise you. And myself. And the way that men are. Because, knowing Bill's reputation, I believed you were lovers. And I believed there were other men too, in your life. And I was jealous because I wanted you for myself. I was deeply angry because I believed you were not as lovely and untouched as you looked and as I wanted you to be.'

The sun shone on her lowered head, turning her hair to gold. Unable to stop himself he stroked it and thrust his fingers through it. Tremors of delight ran through her at his touch.

'I have never been in love with Bill. I have only spoken to him in the hospital, mostly in the dining-room. He has only been friendly to me, he's keen on Nurse Coe.'

Miles looked puzzled. 'But that first day when I met you at your aunt's, she warned me off with almost her first words by saying you were in love with him.'

Helena flashed him a quick, embarrassed glance. 'She—she was mistaken. I—I told her I was in love with a doctor at Trelawny who had no time for me because he was in love with someone else. I didn't say who he was. It was you who jumped to the conclusion that it was Bill.'

They were silent while he thought over what she had said. Rocky lay stretched out at their feet, one ear cocked to listen to what they were saying.

'Who was the doctor, Helena?'

Her cheeks became a warm peach. 'Well, it—it was you, actually.' There was a teasing glint in her eyes. 'But of course, I didn't know you then.'

He lifted her face so that he could look into her eyes.

'And now that you do?'

She lowered her lashes so that they cast shadows on her cheeks. Then she raised her eyes shyly and there was so much love in them that he had no need for a reply.

'It is a strange coincidence,' he said tenderly, 'but I fell in love with you, too, before I really knew you.'

'And now that you do?' she countered with a smile.

'Now that I do, I want more than anything in the world to marry you.'

Her head seemed in a whirl, she did not know whether this was a dream or reality.

'Oh, Miles,' she said in a wondering voice, 'how can you when I've done everything wrong ever since I met you? I—I've always believed that you thought I was hopeless.'

He said on a laugh, 'I do, my love, I do. And that is why I really must take you away from the hospital before you do something dreadful. I have the welfare of my patients to consider.'

'You beast!' She pummelled his chest with angry fists but he captured them and drew her into his arms. Then his mouth silenced her with a kiss that was everything and more than she had ever dreamed that a kiss could be. It was tender and loving, yet deeply passionate with the promise of wonderful things to come.

The sun shone from a cloudless sky and a faint breeze caressed their hair. Everywhere was silent save for a long drawn-out sigh from Rocky, who, contented now, lowered his head and rested it on his paws.

Doctor Nurse Romances

Amongst the intense emotional pressures of modern medical life, doctors and nurses often find romance. Read about their lives and loves in the other three Doctor Nurse titles available this month.

THE CAUTIOUS HEART
by Judith Worthy

As far as Sister Nerys Kent is concerned, nothing could be less hospitable than the great red-dust outback of Western Australia. Nothing, that is, except the reception given her by Dr Hallam Vale, senior partner at the tiny hospital in the mining town of Kolbardi...

THE PROFESSOR'S DAUGHTER
by Leonie Craig

When surgeon Oliver Steele arrives at St Clement's everyone is captivated by his surgical skill and his thoughtfulness for staff and patients alike. Everyone except Sister Sara West, whose encounters with him in her Men's Surgical ward lead her to believe that he's not only Steele by name, but steel by nature, too...

A SURGEON'S LIFE
by Elizabeth Harrison

Leo was recognised to be the most outstanding surgeon at the Central London Hospital. But he was hardly a conventional romantic figure. So who would have guessed that his affair with his frail young secretary Judith — who was threatened by a disabling illness — would turn out to be the greatest love story the hospital have ever known?

Mills & Boon
the rose of romance

Mills & Boon

4 Doctor Nurse Romances
FREE

Coping with the daily tragedies and ordeals of a busy hospital, and sharing the satisfaction of a difficult job well done, people find themselves unexpectedly drawn together. Mills & Boon Doctor Nurse Romances capture perfectly the excitement, the intrigue and the emotions of modern medicine, that so often lead to overwhelming and blissful love. By becoming a regular reader of Mills & Boon Doctor Nurse Romances you can enjoy EIGHT superb new titles every two months plus a whole range of special benefits: your very own personal membership card, a free newsletter packed with recipes, competitions, bargain book offers, plus big cash savings.

**AND an Introductory FREE GIFT for YOU.
Turn over the page for details.**

Fill in and send this coupon back today and we'll send you
4 Introductory
Doctor Nurse Romances yours to keep
FREE

At the same time we will reserve a subscription to Mills & Boon Doctor Nurse Romances for you. Every two months you will receive the latest 8 new titles, delivered direct to your door. You don't pay extra for delivery. Postage and packing is always completely Free. There is no obligation or commitment – you receive books only for as long as you want to.

It's easy! Fill in the coupon below and return it to
MILLS & BOON READER SERVICE, FREEPOST, P.O. BOX 236, CROYDON, SURREY CR9 9EL.

Please note: **READERS IN SOUTH AFRICA** write to Mills & Boon Ltd., Postbag X3010, Randburg 2125, S. Africa.

- - - - - - - - - - - - - - -

FREE BOOKS CERTIFICATE

To: Mills & Boon Reader Service, FREEPOST, P.O. Box 236, Croydon, Surrey CR9 9EL.

Please send me, free and without obligation, four Dr. Nurse Romances, and reserve a Reader Service Subscription for me. If I decide to subscribe I shall receive, following my free parcel of books, eight new Dr. Nurse Romances every two months for £8.00, post and packing free. If I decide not to subscribe, I shall write to you within 10 days. The free books are mine to keep in any case. I understand that I may cancel my subscription at any time simply by writing to you. I am over 18 years of age.
Please write in BLOCK CAPITALS.

Name _____

Address _____

_____

_____ Postcode _____

SEND NO MONEY — TAKE NO RISKS

Remember, postcodes speed delivery Offer applies in UK only and is not valid to present subscribers. Mills & Boon reserve the right to exercise discretion in granting membership. If price changes are necessary you will be notified. Offer expires 31st December 1984.

8DN

EP11D